The Quilt Show Caper

Mary Devlin Lynch
and
Debbie Devlin Zook
with
Beth Devlin-Keune

This is a work of fiction. Names, characters, places, and incidents are the products of the authors' imaginations or are used fictitiously. Any resemblance to actual events, locales, or persons, living or dead, is entirely coincidental.

Published by *DevlinsBooks*

This book is dedicated to three amazing quilters who were commissioned to create a special quilt for Mary's recent birthday. Our youngest sister, Beth, worked with a talented friend to design the "family hands" quilt which has the handprints of every member of our immediate family appliquéd on top. We want to recognize and thank these talented women who created this family heirloom quilt for us: Carla Higgins, Edna Crane, and Dot Fabian.
(A color photo can be found on our website at www.devlinsbooks.com.)

One

"Ladies, please come to order!" Queenie absentmindedly picked up a pair of scissors and tapped them against her plastic water bottle, producing a funny twanging sound. She frowned at the bottle, then shrugged and addressed the group.

"Today's meeting is going to be a special one. We won't be doing one of our normal charity projects." She paused while we stared at her in disbelief. "Oh, we'll be doing charity work, but it'll be a very special assignment." She was grinning from ear to ear and this was not like Queenie. It takes quite a bit to impress her.

We waited in curious anticipation. Once a month, our weekly meeting is devoted to creating pieces to donate to worthy causes. Queenie receives requests from local organizations and then chooses a relatively simple project like pillowcases, throw pillows, lap robes, or baby quilts. As a group, we can produce at least a dozen of anything in our Saturday session. It always feels good to give back to our community using our quilting skills. This was the first time since I've been a member that our charity work has been usurped! *What's up with that?*

"I know it's a shock, but fear not, for we have big news, quilters!" Another dramatic pause, but we waited her out.

I kept an eye on Brittany. Our youngest quilter and mother of two preschoolers, Brittany Bartlett is a tiny pixie of a girl, complete with a cap of short brown hair and brown eyes. Her youngest is turning four soon and the older one will start kindergarten this fall. Since her husband usually has Saturdays off, she's able to get a break from her household and child-rearing duties at least for a couple of hours by joining us at Queenie's for the guild meetings. She also does everything at lightning speed and has had a time learning that Queenie will not be rushed when she's having a moment. I prayed she wouldn't interrupt; it never helped.

"The Mayor has asked us to host … a quilt show!" Queenie announced. "In approximately one month."

The room erupted in choruses of "Wow!" and "Oh boy!" and "OMG!" (Brittany). To restore silence, she raised a perfectly manicured, ring-bedazzled hand. "Please, let me continue.

"I told her I was certain you'd all be delighted." I joined a new round of enthusiastic murmurs and nods. "But seriously, ladies, this is going to be a lot of fun but it's also going to be a lot of work. Sandy has asked us to do this to help fund the high school's extracurricular activities." She paused. "The school budget, as some of you know, is being cut every year. The first things to go are extracurricular activities like band trips, art classes, and sports, which seem unnecessary to the powers that be but are really important to the kids."

"Yeah, the band was invited to the State finals this year but can't afford to go!" Judy chimed in.

There were nods, especially from the moms in the group. I had graduated from Cutler High and so had my Zoey so I was thrilled to help.

"We anticipate quilters coming in from out of town and hope the show will also bring in business to our local hotels, restaurants, and such." She raised a perfectly shaped reddish-brown eyebrow. "Maybe a few people will even stop by my quilt shop!"

We all chuckled appreciatively. It sure sounded like a win-win all around.

Queenie handed out packets of papers. She peered at us over her bifocals.

"This is all preliminary, of course, since we're just getting started. We'll be going over the first page now, but there are additional pages for each assignment." She paused to let that information sink in. "Now, so you know, these are just my first random thoughts on how this should go, but I'm open to your ideas as well. As you see, the first item is the location of the show. The mayor has secured the use of the Armory."

I joined the others in another gasp of surprise. The Armory on Route 642 outside of town was a vast empty space usually filled with the drab greens and browns of the high school ROTC during the week and the Army reservists on the weekends.

Sandy Tressler, our mayor, must have twisted a few arms on this one. Electing a 30-something woman was proving to be a great idea for our little town.

"The second item on your sheet is the date, exactly four weeks from today. I know it's relatively short notice, but it was the only weekend for the next few months that the reservists will be out of town on maneuvers so that we can use the Armory."

Queenie McQuinn, the President of Cutler Quilt Guild Number One, is also a former actress, which doesn't appear to be a profession one can easily leave behind. She runs Queenie's Quilt Shop and our guild with all the command and gusto of her artistic persona. Given a chance to put on a show, you'd better believe she will!

And if that isn't enough, her physical appearance is also rather intimidating. Queenie is a tall, large-framed woman, with a pile of orange-red hair and pale blue eyes. Her wardrobe tends toward long, brightly colored tunics with pockets, worn with straight-leg black pants or tights. The pockets often bulge with measuring tape, pins, and thread. Today's top was cornflower blue with silver buttons and her earrings were large silver hoops.

I thought to myself that it was a good thing the quilters were used to taking direction from her because she would be all over this show and issuing orders like a field marshal.

I wasn't wrong.

"Next you will see an outline of assignments. Judy, you'll be designing the floor plan and space layout."

Judy Smythin's eyes went wide. She works as a cashier at Miller's Drug Store and the sum total of her design experience is setting up the displays in their storefront windows.

"Brittany, you'll work with Judy on that and also help us keep track of expenses."

Brittany Bartlett is our fearless stay-at-home mom, who has learned to make use of every square foot of space in her small home and make every dollar count, gave her a thumbs-up. She and Judy exchanged nods and Judy visibly relaxed.

"Harriet, Sarah, you will work with me on assigning categories, displaying the quilts, and assist in the judging. That's as far as I've gotten on that but we'll have to figure out prizes, etc. Of course, there must be a blue ribbon!"

Harriet and Sarah Moore, twin sisters who are both retired school teachers and extraordinary quilters, beamed at Queenie.

And that left me. I held my breath and decided not to look at the sheet. *Dear Lord, don't let her put me in charge of advertising, not on the internet anyway!*

"Miranda, your assignment is to invite some quilters to the show who will attract a crowd. Obviously, it would be great if we could get either Lydia Peterson or Marcia Travis. Either one of their antique quilts would be a draw. And there are also several regional quilters with good reputations." She glanced at me. "I started a list and it's in your packet." Then she added, "I'll also ask you to take charge of the cash raffle from start to finish." She gave me an elegant hand wave. "That means everything from getting the tickets printed to selling them before and during the show, any way you can."

Whew! That's a relief. As head librarian of the Cutler Community Library, I can form a relatively decent sentence and draft a polite email with the best of them. And I was already mentally preparing a checklist of items I'd need to set up the cash raffle. We do them at the library so this was no problem for me.

Just like the school, every year when the town council is looking for items in the budget to cut, the library ultimately ends up taking a hit. We do special events throughout the year, including raffles, to supplement our budget. The budget basically pays for staff salaries and building operation, from a nuts-and-bolts viewpoint, but leaves very little for purchasing new books, supplies, and equipment. I made a mental note to call James down at the print shop about the raffle tickets as soon as I got home.

Queenie glanced at her plastic bottle, shook her head and then raised a hand to get our attention and address the concerned looks on everyone's faces. Once the original excitement started to wane, I'm sure I wasn't the only one wondering how we could pull this off in one month.

"Ladies, I'm sure you'll all be relieved to hear that we won't be in this alone." She took off her bifocals and dropped them back to their permanent place hanging by a silver beaded chain around her neck and resting on her ample bosom, joining a second pair, magnifying glasses, which she uses when threading needles or doing close-up finish work on a quilted piece.

"We'll have lots of help. Sandy has asked students from the high school art department and computer lab to create advertising posters, internet and newspaper ads, etc. Students in the building trades at the Tech School are being asked to build frames to display the quilts, and the electrical engineering students will add some additional temporary lighting fixtures to the Armory. We will have more kids available for setup, teardown, and everything in between."

I heard one large combined sigh of relief from the group.

"You will note at the bottom of the sheet that I'm asking each of you to display a piece of your own work. Think about it and let me know which pieces you have chosen. These will, of course, be for display only and, sorry, but you cannot win a prize."

The noise level rose.

"Just a moment, ladies, please, we're almost finished. This is early days, of course, and we'll be developing this as we go." She paused. "While the show is going on, each of you will need to be available to work registration, and collect or sell show tickets and raffle tickets. Therefore, we all need to plan on being there the entire time so make arrangements now if possible. Anyone with questions or concerns, stay behind and see me after." Her head moved up and down in her trademark dismissive nod without a hair moving on her head. That always fascinated me with my light flyaway hair; Queenie never had a tendril out of place.

One month! Not much time! This was the tenor of the comments as we took off to begin our tasks. At least I did. Brit and Judy headed toward Queenie to get further instructions. Before the door closed behind me, I heard her tell Judy she would have a key to the Armory later and suggest that she and Brit meet her there. I was curious to see the Armory myself but I knew I'd be spending time there soon and decided it might be best to stay out of the way of those folks actually working the space.

I headed home to start my own, much simpler, tasks.

Word quickly spread through the town. With his large extended family, it didn't take long for him to find out. While others might have been excited about the show, all he saw was dollar signs. A room full of people and a box full of cash. Seemed like easy pickings for someone who had stolen before. He'd be in and out before they knew he was there. Those old ladies wouldn't know what hit them.

Two

I couldn't stop smiling all the way home. In Cutler, with its population of around 3,000, this was going to be a very big deal. Everyone in town would be involved or taking advantage of the influx of people for our small businesses. A few years back, as with so many small towns with no direct exit off the interstate, downtown Cutler was dying.

Thanks to Sandy Tressler, our dynamic young mayor, and the town council, it was undergoing revitalization. Together, they had instituted plans to bring businesses and traffic back to town. The results were clear in the new shops that filled almost all of the previously deserted commercial spaces. The quilt show was another of Mayor Tressler's creative ideas to bring attention to Cutler; that was enough to make me smile.

I pulled into my garage and walked around the back of the house to the kitchen door. This is my usual entrance and also the one used by most of my visitors. Very rarely does anyone come to my front door. I'm not sure why; I never gave it much thought. Maybe because everyone knows that if I'm home I'm either in the kitchen or in my office/sewing room that's located at the back of the house.

Over the years, my late husband, Harry, remodeled almost every room in this house. He turned our third bedroom into an office and sewing room for me. At first, we thought it might have been a mistake to take away the third bedroom but, since we had remained a family of three, it worked.

We purchased the classic ranch back when they were popular and when small housing developments were popping up around the outskirts of town. We chose ours because it was close enough that Zoey could walk to school.

So now there are two bedrooms. Zoey's room looks about the same as it did when she was in high school. Someday maybe I'll change it up a bit, or at least put one of my quilts on the double bed to surprise her. In our bedroom, Harry added a master bathroom. It wasn't long after Zoey was born he realized that with two women in the house we would definitely need a second bathroom.

I entered through the kitchen door, and shouted as I always did, "Harry, I'm home!"

I was greeted with a "*Meow*" and heard a faint thud as my chunky cat jumped down from his spot on the leather recliner. He entered the kitchen and wound himself around my legs, purring.

"There you are, Harry. How's it goin'? I have a lot to tell you. The Quilt Guild is sponsoring a quilt show in a month. Can you believe it? Queenie hasn't given us much time to prepare."

Leaving him to absorb the news, I gave him a little scratch on the head and went back the hallway to my room. While I changed into my comfy clothes, Harry made his way to his recliner. When I came back, I sat down in my chair next to his and pulled a pencil and pad from the drawer in the small table located between the two chairs. I wrote "Quilt Show—To-Do List" at the top.

I know you're curious and we all remember what curiosity did to *that* cat—how, you ask, did I wind up with a cat named after my husband?

When my Harry died as the result of a hunting accident, I'd gone into a state of shock. All of our hopes and dreams and plans were gone in a split second. I was struggling to adjust. One evening, as I went to the kitchen to heat up the remainder of a casserole provided by one of my friends, I heard scratching at the back door.

I opened it and a slightly bedraggled gray and white cat walked in as if he owned the place, padded straight through to the living room, and jumped up onto Harry's recliner. I followed.

"You don't live here, cat," I said, or something to that effect.

The cat, who clearly intended to nap, opened his eyes and winked at me, just like my Harry used to do. *Seriously.* And that's the short version of how Harry the cat came into my life.

Now back to my list. I perused Queenie's packet again. The amount of detail she had pulled together already was impressive.

The maximum occupancy limit for the Armory is 500 people. With our entry fee of $20 a person, our goal was $10,000, which seemed realistic if not conservative. We would expect a lot of traffic throughout the course of the day so maybe we could get closer to 1,000. That would be amazing.

I found the preliminary information about the raffle and whistled. While the rest of us were putting our personal quilting projects on hold for the duration and volunteering our time, Queenie had gone above and beyond, donating a $3,500 Husqvarna sewing/quilting machine as a door prize!

She had set a price of $10 a ticket so I immediately decided to splurge and buy 20 for myself. I've been drooling over the higher-end machines in her shop since it opened. I make do with my simple model but, in my heart, I want an extravagant computer-programmable beauty. I could actually afford to buy one but I am a Scot by blood and a thrifty sort by habit. Maybe it's the thrill of getting a bargain; I rarely buy anything that's not on sale. So winning it would be a dream come true! And, no, the fact that I would be printing the tickets and promoting their sale did not constitute a conflict of interest as far as I was concerned. Queenie would be drawing the name of the winner, not me.

I quickly did the math. We'd need to sell 350 tickets for her to break even so maybe I'd print a thousand? Even though it was Saturday afternoon, I knew James Kelley would be in his little print/copy/shipping shop, which is attached to his home. He answered on the first ring.

"James, it's Miranda Hathaway. How are you?"

"Hey, Miranda. I'm great! What can I do for ya?"

"How's Jessie doing?"

"Good. She's gonna be teaching fifth grade this year." He chuckled. "Those second-graders were too much for her to handle."

"I hear that. Now, the reason I called is to get some raffle tickets printed for a quilt show the guild is sponsoring next month."

"Hey, I know something about that. Sandy has been one of Jessie's best friends since they were kids. They had their heads together over at the house the other night."

"Right, and here's the deal. Queenie's donating a $3,500 Husqvarna machine. She wants the tickets to be $10 each."

"Well, shoot, Miranda, you don't need anything special then. I'd recommend that you get a roll of basic drawing tickets with numbers and spaces for names on each one. I'm thinkin' maybe a couple thousand."

"To be honest, James, I don't have a clue how many I need."

He continued. "Well, show's at the Armory, right? So, if 400 to 500 people show up and each buys two tickets, there's a thousand. Now you're gonna sell some around town and whatnot. Normally, I sell them at $40 a roll of a thousand, but I can let you have the two thousand for $50, if that'll help."

"That's fantastic. So you have these at the shop?"

"Yup. Stop by and pick 'em up anytime."

I sighed in relief. "Thanks for making this so easy. And tell Jessie I was asking after her, okay?"

"Will do. Take care now."

Glancing over at Harry, who was pretending to nap, I pumped my arm in the air and congratulated myself. "*Boom*, Harry, the raffle is under way! Am I good or what?"

He rolled over onto his back and laughed his cat laugh. "*Eck, eck, eck.*"

"Well, that's enough work for one day. How about we order a pizza from Main Street to celebrate?"

His ears perked up. "*Yeow*."

And so we did.

Three

The next day being Sunday, Harry and I slept in a bit. We were drinking coffee and reading the paper, well, at least one of us was while the other supervised, when the phone rang.

I smiled when I saw ZOEY on the screen. My daughter calls me fairly often. We're as close as we can be considering that we are living in different states. I hold the fort in Cutler while she lives in Boston. My overachiever daughter got her bachelor's at 21, her master's at 23, and will be finishing up her Ph.D. in English Literature before she turns 26. While I'm bragging on her, she's also beautiful with her father's thick dark wavy hair (mine is light brown and tends to be on the thin side) and height (she towered over me by about six inches or so). She did get my green eyes, which I think are my best feature. So she made out pretty well in the genetics sweepstakes.

"Hey, Mom. What's happening?"

"And good morning to you, too, sweetheart!" I heard laughter at the other end of the line.

"Everything's good here. How are things in Boston?"

"Great, really great!" She cleared her throat and I knew something big was coming. "Mom, I want to tell you something and I know you'll be supportive." She emphasized this last part in a way that I recognized as a warning that I had better be supportive. "Michael and I are thinking of moving in together. We spend all of our time at each other's places now and we could save the extra money for wedding expenses next year."

She had clearly rehearsed her speech and, even though I understood why she'd think I would be opposed, it pained me that she felt she had to sell me on this idea. I knew they were basically living together already and I'm okay with that.

Sure, when I was dating her father, we each lived with out parents until our wedding day. But I know that doesn't work for everyone. There are a lot of surprises, not all of them happy surprises, when you move in with someone and I think that might explain today's high divorce rate.

"Zoey, I'm okay with it. I realize that times have changed. I can understand how expensive it is to maintain two condos in Boston. Now that I've come to know Michael, I know he loves you and takes good care of you. That's all that ever matters to me."

"Thanks for understanding, Mom. You're the best." I heard her sigh of relief. "So what have you been up to?"

"Well, since you asked. We're having a quilt show next month! It's gonna be held at the old Armory out on 642 and we're hoping the guild can raise a bunch of money for the school to use for their extracurricular activities."

"Wow, are you serious? That sounds like a lot to accomplish in a month. But the school's never had enough funding. Even when I was there, it seemed like programs were getting eliminated every year. Remember how upset I was when they cut Debate Club? It's just terrible."

"I know. Judy mentioned today that he band can't afford to go to State finals this year. Diane's been saying that the baseball team needs some new equipment. And the last time I went to a football game, even the Cougar's mascot costume looked pretty ragged." I added.

"Well, I think this is a great idea. Tell me the date."

"It's Saturday, June 15."

I heard a click as she checked her calendar. "Oh, darn it." I could hear her pouting through the phone. "Michael has a business dinner thing on that Friday night and I promised to go. And I have a meeting with my advisor on the final edits to my thesis on Saturday morning."

"Really, Zoey? You're almost finished?"

"Yes and no. If Barbara approves these last changes then I think the editing is done, but I still have to pull it all together. So it's gonna be a couple more months, but I'm getting close."

"Well, that's a meeting you shouldn't miss. By the way, I don't tell you often enough how proud I am of you, Zoey."

"Thanks, Mom."

"I'm sorry you'll miss the quilt show, honey. But I'll be sure to fill you in as things progress here."

"It's just not fair. Nothing exciting ever happened in Cutler when I lived there."

I laughed out loud at her childish sulk.

"I agree that exciting things don't happen around here very often. In all my years, I can only remember two—the big bank heist and the quilt ripper." I tried to suppress a giggle but Zoey started to laugh.

"Oh my gosh, I almost forgot about the old man who took his shotgun to the bank and shot holes in his safe deposit box after he lost his key and the bank manager refused to open the box for him. How is Old Rafe these days?"

"I believe he lives in a retirement village over in Danville, and I'm pretty sure they took his shotgun away from him permanently."

"And the quilt ripper. Do you keep in touch with Amy? After all, if it weren't for her Gabe would have never come to Cutler and you would never have met and he wouldn't be your 'main squeeze' these days."

Zoey takes great delight in coming up with different ways of expressing Gabe's and my connection because "boyfriend" simply seems silly at our ages. So far, the list includes "significant other," "gentleman caller," "beau," "plus one," "suitor," "man friend," "swain," and now "main squeeze." I'm sure she's working from a list she found somewhere to tease me and amuse herself.

"Main squeeze! Where on earth did you hear that one?" I laughed.

"I heard it on an old gangster movie the other night. I've been holding onto it for the next time we spoke."

"Okay, okay. I surrender."

"And how is Gabe? Seriously?"

"He's good but he's been on a case that has had him traveling for the past week. He called a couple of times. Zoey, I know he's a former FBI agent, but I still worry about him. I have no idea if these cases that he works on are dangerous. And, of course, he'd never tell me if they were. Confidentiality and all that!" Realizing that I suddenly sounded awfully whiny, I added brightly, "But the good news is that he's planning on being here to help out with the quilt show!"

"Well, please tell him I said, 'Hi!' And I really do want to come home for a night or two as soon as we can swing it."

"That would be wonderful, sweetheart." I heard a slight beep on the phone.

"Hey, I gotta run, that's Michael calling. We have plans with Olivia and Ali this afternoon. Talk soon. And, Mom, I love you."

"Right back at ya, Zoey. Talk soon."

I made our breakfast with minimal effort: a bowl of cereal for me and a cup of dry cat food for Harry. After clearing the table and loading the dishes into the dishwasher, I went into my office to attack my second task of the day. I didn't anticipate it being much more difficult than the first.

Email seemed to me to be the way to go about my invitations so I went through a couple of websites and finally found an address for Lydia Peterson, our number one targeted quilter.

There was also a picture of her antique medallion quilt. Just FYI, a medallion quilt doesn't mean a medallion or medal is involved. The medallion is a large center block, or picture, with layers of blocks around it. It can be round or square. The outer edges and corners can be whatever the quilter chooses. The most striking thing about Lydia's quilt was how modern it looked, considering it was made in the 1840s!

The white background highlighted the center medallion, a square on point, done all in red as a large basket of flowers. The complexity of the flower arrangement was astonishing. It was bordered in red. Outside the border of the medallion, a floral chain with trailing leaves marched the whole way around. Then a band of red fabric quilted in red bordered it on the outside. I couldn't imagine how long it took to create this masterpiece. I admit freely that my heart beat a little faster at the idea of seeing it up close and in person.

I drafted an invitation, sending out only positive thoughts along with it.

Dear Ms. Peterson,

I would like to extend an invitation to our first Cutler Quilt Show to be held on June 15. We would be honored if you would consider attending as our guest and displaying your medallion quilt. As you may well imagine, the quilters in our small town and local area are quite excited at the prospect of meeting you and seeing your amazing antique quilt. We also anticipate some unique and interesting entries from the nearby Harrisburg and Lancaster areas.

If you choose to join us, we will be pleased to provide accommodations for an overnight stay for your convenience. We look forward to your prompt response by return email or you can call me directly. All contact information is included at the bottom of my note.

Sincerely, Miranda Hathaway, on behalf of Cutler Quilt Guild Number One, Cutler, PA

Next I sent a similar invitation to Marcia Travis, referencing her colonial floral quilt. Her quilt was not quite as unique as Lydia's but it was impressive and almost as antique, dating from the 1850s. Multicolored flowers moved out from a center three-stem bouquet on vines like spider legs. The appliqués were intricate and interesting. The pattern felt a bit more dated than the other quilt. Still, I wouldn't pass up a chance to see it up close!

I didn't mention to the two women that they had both been invited. It wasn't necessary to the invitation. And, of course, there is the fact that they loathe each other. No need to go there right now.

Internet searches provided three more names of accomplished quilters in the Harrisburg and Lancaster areas and I added them to my list.

Sending the remaining invitations was easy after that and I zipped through them. Unlike Lydia and Marcia, most of the others listed in Queenie's extensive packet had their own websites and prominently displayed email addresses.

I made notes on everything that I had done to keep things straight. I'd call Queenie on Monday to report my progress. If everyone responded, we would have about 20 guest quilters and then around 10 quilts from our own collections. They would never mention it but I knew for a fact that the Moore sisters had at least three award-winning quilts of their own.

My stomach grumbled, prompting me to check the refrigerator. It was getting close to dinner time and I had no leftovers so I grabbed my purse and car keys.

"See ya later, Harry. Goin' on a food run."

"*Meow, meow*!" He obviously thought I'd be sharing whatever I brought back so it sounded like he was saying, "Make it fast. I'm hungry, too!"

Just for the record, I usually cook about three nights a week and live on leftovers or salads the other days. When Gabe's here, he often takes over the kitchen which is fine by me. He enjoys cooking while I freely admit that I only cook to eat. If someone else wants to cook for me or take me out to dinner, for that matter, I'm good with that, too.

I walked into Sylvia's Diner and climbed up on one of the stools in front of the counter. The kitchen door swung open and Sylvia bounced over to me.

"Hey there, hon. How ya doin'?"

"I'm great. What're your specials for today?"

"Choice of roasted turkey dinner or ham, green beans, and potatoes. Made 'em all myself."

"I'll go with the turkey dinner. Thanks, Syl."

She disappeared back into the kitchen and I looked around. There were several families in the booths in the back and a few young men seated on the other side of the counter. My eyes wandered back to the stool at the end just inside the door. I half expected to see Andy sitting there in his army fatigues.

Andy Perretta was a veteran who wandered into town and stayed for around six months. He'd seen several tours of combat and watched many of the men in his units die. When he got home to Philadelphia, he had a hard time adjusting to civilian life. So he got up one morning, packed a few things, left a note for his wife, and walked away.

We still don't know how he came to be in Cutler, could have hitchhiked with a trucker or something, I guess, but the town adopted him and kept him safe until he was ready to go home. At last report, Andy and his Marie are expecting and couldn't be happier. Andy now works at the local vets' home with other returning veterans. It's the perfect job for him; he knows better than anyone what it's like to return from service and feel totally disconnected from your life.

I might have been smiling when Sylvia returned with my food containers already bagged and ready to go.

"I know that look. Thinking 'bout Andy, are ya?"

"Just can't help myself. It doesn't seem like it's been a year already since he went home."

"Don't I know it. Every time that bell above the door rings, I think it might be him walkin' in. But he's doin' great from what I hear."

"Their baby should be due any time now."

"You'll let me know when ya hear, right?"

"Absolutely!"

I paid for my supper and said goodbye. As I approached the door, it swung open back at me.

My best friend since elementary school popped inside. "Hello, stranger."

"DeeDee. Fancy meeting you here."

"It's turkey night, isn't it?" She grinned. Diane's not known for her love of cooking any more than I am.

"I held up my bag. "Yep."

Sylvia waved her over to the register. "Your food's ready, Diane."

Diane nodded. :Okay, gotta run. I've got papers to grade."

"Hey, did you hear about the quilt show?"

She smirked. "Honey, there ain't nothin' goes on in this town I don't know about."

I laughed. "Now is that any way for an English teacher to talk?"

She shrugged. "Look, we have to get together and you can tell me all the inside scoop. This is ridiculous."

"I know. I miss you too." I gave her a quick hug and headed home.

Back at the house, I unpacked my dinner and found a small packet of dark meat with a note attached. "For Harry."

"Hey, Harry. Sylvia sent you some turkey."

I heard the thud as he jumped down from the recliner and wandered nonchalantly into the kitchen. He sat down beside his dish and waited. This was another of his Harry habits. As soon as I'd say dinner was almost ready, Harry would come to the kitchen and sit in his place, waiting for the food to appear.

I cut the turkey into small bites on a plate that I placed on the floor next to his water. He waited until I sat down at the table before digging in. His politeness made me smile; my first Harry did that, too.

After dinner, Harry and I passed the rest of the evening watching baseball. I try to keep up with the Red Sox since that's Gabe's favorite team.

Gabe came into my life almost two years ago now. He came to Cutler on a case and he actually infiltrated, yes, infiltrated, our quilt guild as part of his investigation. Fast-forward to today and we are "a couple," albeit long distance for now.

It took me a bit longer than Gabe to realize that we were meant for each other but I eventually figured it out. He's tall, tan, athletic, and affectionate, with crystal blue eyes and an amazing head of white hair. I could go on all day, but the bottom line is that he has given me a second chance at love that I never thought I'd get. Harry and I had been married over 30 years when he died. Then I dated a bit but found no one like my Harry or anything close to what I now share with Gabe.

We're taking it slow because we both have emotional baggage. Gabe has been divorced for over three years now. Harry's been gone about the same length of time.

We talk often and, whenever possible, one of us makes the trek to the other's home. It's a six-hour drive and I must admit I'm not crazy about that part but, when I go to his home in Newton, I do get to spend time with Zoey as well. Gabe usually comes down and spends a long weekend at least once a month.

I was hoping he'd call soon. I watched the baseball game and made some notes about how many hits "Big Papi" had, David Price's pitching performance, and the final score. My Harry was a big baseball fan so I know something about the sport. Now I try to keep an eye on the Sox so I can hold up my end of the conversation when Gabe mentions them.

As soon as the game ended, I stood up and stretched. Harry jumped down and did the same.

"Okay, Harry, that's it for me. I'm off to bed."

"*Neow*."

"Yes, now."

We went to the bedroom and I folded the quilt down to the bottom where Harry immediately curled up in his favorite spot. I crawled into my side and turned off the light. Then I reached over and pulled the opposite pillow down to wrap my arms around as I went to sleep.

My bedding and my own pillowcase may have been changed several times since his last visit but Gabe's hadn't and that was no accident. There was just the faintest scent of his aftershave left.

Four

The next morning, feeling good about my show tasks being well under way, I went about my normal workday routine. I performed my cat staff duties and made sure Harry's dishes were fresh and filled and the litter clean while he supervised.

"So, Harry." I brought him up to speed. "The invitations are on their way. Now I just have to hope for fast responses. Isn't this going to be amazing?"

Harry lifted a paw, swept it clean with his tongue, and then yawned widely.

"Try to curb your excitement!" I patted him on the head. "See ya later."

The Cutler Community Library serves not only as a place for taking out books, reading them, or borrowing a computer, but we also try to bring something extra to the community. Monday is Kid's Day and our noisiest for sure, but also our most enjoyable.

I got in at 9:00, an hour before it started, to make sure we were all set for the small mob of kiddies. Lucy, our only full-time employee and an absolute gem, came through the door right behind me. She's almost as shiny, too, with her bright red hair and blue eyes. Her freckly face is smiling. She looks like a kid herself, but recently celebrated her 35th birthday.

We share a passion for reading and she's taking courses in library management so she may well take my place when I retire as Head Librarian. I think I have a few years left in me but it makes me happy to think that we have someone already in place who loves the library as much as I do.

"Mornin', Luce."

"Good morning, Miranda." She pulled a big box of animal crackers from her tote bag. We walked over to the Kiddie Corner together. She put the box on the shelf and picked up a couple of books that had been placed on the chair where the volunteer would sit. "These are the books for this morning."

I glanced at the titles. "It looks like we're good to go!"

"We have a couple of extra juice boxes in the refrigerator, too, in case anyone forgets theirs."

"Who's reading today?"

"Brittany."

We grinned at each other.

"I know what you're thinking." Lucy said. "She can be a handful but she's wonderful with the children and her two are very well behaved."

Brit's a bit different from the rest of us and not just because she's considerably younger; as we locals say, she's got a mouth on her. She's also been known to use language that the rest of us wouldn't, at least not in public. I've come to understand that she has four older brothers and in order to be heard in her family home, she had to learn to speak up.

And, apparently, she picked up some of her more colorful language from those same older brothers.

But her youthful enthusiasm and energy is contagious and she's a really hard worker. She's been volunteering at the library almost weekly since her kids were babies. She'd chosen the books she would read. Brittany is a favorite reader because she uses different voices for the characters. Her audience would be about 15 kids ranging from three to five years old. The library staff, including me, could often be found hovering around the doorway, presumably keeping an eye on the desk, but also listening to Brittany read.

"Outstanding."

"I know." She grinned at me, and then looked at her watch. "Hmm. William seems to be running late. I'll just unlock down here and shelve a few books 'til he gets in."

I nodded. "Thanks, Lucy. If he isn't here by 9:30 or so, give him a call to make sure there's nothing wrong."

"No worries."

I went to the breakroom, filled the water well on the single-cup coffee maker and made myself a mug of coffee. We used to have a glass pot sitting on a hot plate all day, getting thicker by the minute. Those days, we threw away almost as much as we drank. In about two minutes, I was on my way up the stairs to my office with a nice strong fresh cup.

Mondays start out slow and pick up speed as the day goes on. That meant I actually had time to look at the monthly calendar. My staff already had several events planned, but I had a couple of ideas to add. I made some notes to give to

Lucy and then I'd let her take charge. There are some things that I delegate and the calendar of events is one of them. I know that William and Janie, our trusty part-timers, will give her a hand with anything she needs.

My cell phone rang about half an hour later. I don't often answer it at work but I make exceptions for Gabe or Zoey.

"Hi there."

"Good morning, sunshine."

The sound of Gabe's deep voice sent warm tingles through my body. "So how are you?"

"Honestly? Tired. I got back in town late last night and wanted to call you as soon as I could. And, unfortunately, I have to leave again tomorrow. I could be gone for a week or more."

"I was hoping you were going to say you were coming to Cutler this weekend." I didn't try to hide my disappointment.

"I was hoping to."

When I heard the same disappointment in his voice, I decided to stop pouting and be a grown-up. "You would be very welcome," I answered warmly.

I could almost hear him smiling through the phone. "So what's new in Cutler?"

I told him about the quilt show.

"You sound excited."

"Oh, I am, Gabe. You know how much fun it is to see other people's work and get to talk to people who share the same passions you do."

He chuckled. "I do. I trust there will be machine-quilted pieces as well as displays of hand-quilting?" Gabe did machine quilting for us at the guild so that's his particular quilting passion.

"Oh, I'm sure, because Queenie and the twins are working on the categories for judging. And since the guild is sponsoring the show, I know Queenie will have a display of items from her shop, including several quilting machines. I doubt that she takes the 12-footer to the Armory but she'll at least probably have a picture of it.

"And get this, she's donated a Husqvarna with a price tag of $3,500 for the raffle, which I happen to be in charge of, by the way!"

"When is this?"

"A month from last Saturday. June 15."

"I'll be there. I'm gonna put that on my calendar now."

"I was hoping you'd say that." I took a breath. "At least I know I'll see you then."

He was quiet for a moment. "If not sooner."

"Sooner would be good, too," I responded softly.

"Okay, I'd better get moving. I have some paperwork to finish up and laundry to do before I pack up again. And I'm having dinner with Kevin tonight."

"How's he doin'?"

"No idea, that's why I told him to be sure to be home for dinner, so I can find out what he's been up to. Well, I should run. Have a good week, sweetheart."

"Back at you, big guy!" I tried to lighten the mood and heard him laugh as I clicked off the phone.

I had no excuse for feeling blue, I reminded myself. We were grown-ups and we each had our jobs and responsibilities, but Gabe's might actually be dangerous. I know he still has contacts at the FBI and I also know that he's done some surveillance work for them over the years. What I don't know is whether that puts him in danger or not.

I walked to my window and took in the view of downtown Cutler. From the second floor of the library, I could see the quilt shop, the wine shop, and a few other shops along the main street. I watched colorful figures bustling about as people hurried along to work or shop. I saw several moms holding hands of children as they crossed the street and headed to the front door of the library. Then I spotted Brittany with her kids running up the front steps. My smile returned.

Even if Gabe wasn't here right now, I knew I was lucky to have him in my life. The odds sure were against someone like him showing up in Cutler; the odds that we would have a jewel thief in town were also extremely high. Gabe was hired to find the thief who had stolen jewelry that was hidden in antique quilted items inherited by two families in our community. We'd nicknamed the thief the "Quilt Ripper." The ladies of the guild had gotten involved, as well as the local police department. It was the most exciting thing to happen in Cutler in, well, probably decades.

While it's very different from the life he has led, Gabe understands that I'm a small-town girl. He's lived in several different places, traveled all over the world, and now lives about twenty minutes away from Zoey in Newton, Mass. As our relationship has developed, he's never once complained about the six hours between us or asked me to think about moving. With my Zoey there, I admit it would be a fair question.

I suppose you could say that there's nothing to hold me here. Technically, that's true, but emotionally, not so much. I live in the house Harry and I bought together before Zoey was born. I work at the same library I haunted regularly as a child. Diane Murphy has been my best friend since first grade and she lives just a few blocks from me. I know almost all of the folks in this town and their parents and their kids. My roots are so deep I think I might die if they were torn out. I simply don't want to live anywhere else.

Our relationship may be moving forward at a glacierlike speed but we're old enough to appreciate what we've found in each other. Although Gabe's son, Kevin, is in his late twenties, he's still trying to "find himself." My daughter is almost 26 and knows exactly where she's going but isn't quite there yet. I'm a widow and he's divorced. We both had lives before we got here and each have the scars to prove it. We're being careful with this second chance we've been given.

In my wildest dreams, Gabe would move to Cutler. There, I said it out loud, well almost. If he did, we would be living together, so I'd be a real hypocrite to tell Zoey it's wrong for her and Michael.

The way I see it, Cutler is only about an hour from Harrisburg and two hours from Philadelphia. So Gabe could continue his P.I. work from here, right? Okay, I might have given it some thought, just a little.

Five

It was a good thing I was so busy with the quilt show because Gabe didn't make the next weekend or even the next. Acceptances for the quilt show presenters flew in and I responded with thank you emails. There were phone calls and impromptu meetings as I helped Judy and Brit out with the logistics at the Armory.

My raffle ticket sales were going strong. James had refused to accept payment for the two rolls of tickets when I picked them up. He said that since he had two kids at the school, he and his wife had decided to donate them. So I went to about every store in town, handing out loops of tickets for them to sell. Some shops had called me for more.

Before I knew it, we were having our last meeting before the show. Queenie called us to order in her usual way, tapping her scissors against whatever was in front of her, in this case a glass jar containing buttons which made quite a satisfying *clunk, clunk, clunk.* She smiled and tapped it again. *Clunk.*

"Ladies, please come to order. With just a week to go, we have a lot to discuss. First, let's hear from Miranda about the acceptances from the quilters she has invited."

"I have acceptances from several award-winning quilters" I looked at my notepad, "including Betsy Ferguson, Carrie Hilpon, and Georgia McIntosh." I added, "I still haven't heard from Lydia Peterson or Marcia Travis. But I had a call from Amy Truehorn from Lancaster. She has a spectacular bargello she's going to enter and mentioned that a friend would also like to bring her quilt, which is an original variation of the Ohio Star design. It seems that these two ladies travel together everywhere.

"And," I winked at Queenie and announced, "Queenie is showing her grandmother's gorgeous log cabin. So it's going to be fabulous!" My enthusiasm spilled over and I got a round of applause. "Oh, and the raffle tickets are selling great, all over town!"

"Thanks, Miranda. Now let's hear from Judy on the setup at the Armory."

"We're planning displays for 24 quilts. There may be more quilts but some quilters prefer to bring their own displays. The mounting frames and display tables we provide will be set up in four rows," Judy began.

Brittany broke in, throwing her arms up in the air. "And the frames are being made by the Tech School boys from scraps donated by Anderson's Lumber Yard. And the tables are being loaned to us by St. Joe's and St. Aloysius churches for free!"

A round of spontaneous applause broke out as she and Judy high-fived each other.

Judy continued, "I'd like to ask everyone to show up on Thursday afternoon around 3:00 to help the kids set up the tables and display frames. As I understand, most of the quilters will be arriving on Friday, so that they're ready to go first thing on Saturday." She looked at me.

"Yes, most of the women I've talked to want to be here on Friday to set up and we've helped with their reservations for Friday night. The Travel Inn is giving us a group rate for that one night. Most of the quilters plan to pack up and leave after the show ends on Saturday afternoon."

Queenie nodded her approval and then waved a hand.

"Okay, okay. Good work. Moving on to the advertising ..." Queenie pulled up her bifocals and scanned her notes. "I'm sure you've seen the ads that are running in the newspaper, the posters around town, and our internet ad is running on …" she looked down again, "… Facebook and Twitter. It's also posted, as I understand it, on several quilting sites that promote shows, including *Quilting News* and *Quilting Today*."

Somehow she made that whole spiel sound like a question and several of the ladies stifled chuckles at Queenie's obvious lack of familiarity with social media. I wasn't one of them. Let me just say, I've seen Facebook but I'm not on it, despite Zoey's constant nagging. And I won't be tweeting anything any time soon.

Queenie smiled wryly. "And if you want to know any more about that, contact Peter Broodman, our go-to guy at the high school for this technical stuff.

"Moving on to the actual show logistics, we will have two cashboxes, one for admission tickets and one for raffle tickets. But I'd like to have three people at the front table at all times. I know there might be some slack times but we need to be able to control how people are entering the Armory all day."

Brittany waved her hand in the air like she was back in grade school.

"Yes, Brittany?"

"After of our tour of the Armory, you all know that it basically looks like an airplane hangar, which it might have actually been at some point. Anyway, Judy and I have been talking and we think we should open the doors at one end and keep the other end closed up. With that said, I asked the shop teacher to put up some temporary walls just inside the entrance we're using to funnel people toward the center where the ticket tables will be set up." She giggled. "That will also keep them from sneaking a peek at the quilts before they pay their money."

Queenie's eyebrows shot up in surprise. "Excellent. Great thinking! Well done, you two! So, before we move on, remember to be there at 3:00 on Thursday to supervise the setup of all the tables and display frames. Judy and Brittany will have a floor plan printed up and that should make it go smoothly. I'm also counting on each of you to take a turn at the tables on Saturday. Any volunteers for the 10:00 to noon shift?"

Judy, Brittany, and I raised our hands.

I added, "Queenie, there's a good chance that Gabe is coming down for the weekend and I'm sure he'd love to help if we need him."

"It's great to know we have extra hands on site." Queenie beamed at me. "I'm thinking that as Sarah, Harriet, and I will be doing the judging a bit later, we should be able to be out front from noon to 2:00. So we'll need to fill in from 2:00 to 4:00."

"I'm planning on being around all afternoon, so I don't mind working that last shift," Brittany spoke up.

Judy agreed. "I'm planning on being there, too."

I nodded. "Looks like the 10:00 to 12:00 team can help out from 2:00 to 4:00 as well."

"And we'll relieve here and there," Harriet began, "if someone needs a break." Sarah finished.

This is how the twins work. Harriet is about three minutes older and therefore always takes the lead, and Sarah is quick to follow. Come to think of it, I don't think I've ever heard Sarah start a sentence without prompting from Harriet, which I'm sure isn't possible since she was a high school teacher for over 35 years.

"Thanks, ladies, looks like we've got it covered. As for the Quilt Shop, I've made arrangements with my dear friend, Julia Carson, who, as you all know, is an excellent quilter and taught Home Economics at the school before it was eliminated from the curriculum." Queenie paused as we all nodded. "She has agreed to work the shop on Friday and Saturday. We're hoping our visitors will shop downtown before or after the show.

"At my shop display at the Armory, I will have a couple of sewing and quilting machines, fabrics, etc., with coupons for 10% off any purchases at the show or shop on Friday and

Saturday. We'll be open from 10:00 until 8:00 both days." She paused to catch her breath. "I've had James print up special discount cards with my logo."

Then she moved on. "As to the quilt entries, we seem to be well on our way." She frowned. "As you know, we have had to reject several quilts as unsuitable for display. I have nothing more to say about that."

We all knew she was talking about Laura Jenkins and her sad quilts. To say she's a bit of an odd duck would be a kindness. She had submitted an heirloom quilt to Queenie for inclusion in our calendar a couple of years ago.

The calendar was one of the Guild's charity ventures, but it's been discontinued since Judy Smythin and her cousin, Taylor Perryman, had featured items that became the targets of a thief. That's another story but, basically, Queenie had been forced to reject Laura's dirty, worn quilt and the woman was more than miffed.

We were all desperately hoping she wouldn't turn up with an entry for the show, but she did. When we were gathered at the shop for our guild meeting last Saturday, she brought in three quilts. One was the same heirloom piece she had tried to include in the calendar and the other two appeared newer but still in the same neglected state.

When she marched in and placed the quilts on one of our worktables, I was struggling to think of something nice to say, as I expect the others were, too. Awkward would be an understatement. Queenie took charge of Laura and took her into the back office space, no doubt trying to spare her further humiliation. I did not envy Queenie the task of rejecting the woman's pieces one more time.

Master quilter and kindhearted soul that she is, Queenie told us after Laura left (as in stormed out and slammed the door) that she'd gently suggested we could use the antique piece to highlight restoration and cleaning techniques. Laura was outraged and that's putting it mildly. She departed with her quilts but not before turning the air blue around her. She blasted all of us for treating her unfairly and pointed a finger at Judy. There was a collective sigh as the door slammed.

I honestly think that we've gone above and beyond to be kind to Laura, but she's frankly a very sloppy quilter and a nasty person. It's not unusual for amateur quilters to stop by on Saturdays to watch us work or to ask questions. And there's not an experienced quilter I know who wouldn't take the time to give a lesson or two. And believe me when I say that I certainly don't put myself in the expert category. I'm still fairly new to this and have a lot to learn myself. My work is basic at best but I do love it! The trouble is that there's not much you can teach someone who thinks they already know more than you do.

After a moment of quiet, as we all reflected on Laura and her quilts, Queenie brought us back to the matters at hand by clearing her throat.

"We will have room for a few more quilts if anyone else turns up. I trust you are all prepared with your own pieces. If you bring them Thursday, we can get them set up as well."

She pointed her finger at each of us in turn and we announced our entries. Sarah and Harriet each had some stunning variations on tumbling blocks, Brittany had an adorable sailboat quilt she'd made for the kids, Judy had a crazy quilt she had worked long and hard on, and I stated that I was going with the Dresden Plate that I thought was my best work so far.

Queenie declared, "Good choices all around."

We all breathed a sigh of relief.

He couldn't believe his luck. When his name was announced over the loudspeaker, he figured he was in trouble. But the other guys were all goody two shoes so that was nothing new. He kept his cool. He'd been chosen to help out at the quilt show at the Armory next Saturday. All he had to do was show up Thursday afternoon to help set up and come back again on Saturday at the end to help tear down. *Perfect!*

Six

Sunday afternoon, I was on the phone with Zoey, listening patiently to a summary of her dissertation, the title of which is “Significance of the Feminist Author From the Nineteenth Century to the Twentieth Century.” She’s hoping to become a full professor in the English Literature Department at Boston University.

I was concentrating so hard on trying to follow her monologue that I didn’t realize immediately that my phone was beeping with another call. I don’t usually switch over on people but the name came up as “Marcia Travis.”

“Oh, Zoey, honey, I hate to interrupt but I have to take this call. It’s one of the quilters we’re desperate to get for the show. I’ll call you back.”

She laughed. “And you’re desperate to get away from hearing about my paper ad nauseum. It’s okay. Talk later. ’Bye, Mom!”

I do love that kid. I quickly pushed the switch button and said, “Hello.”

Marcia introduced herself and asked, quite pleasantly, if she could come to the show. She apologized for not responding sooner. Then she went on to explain that she’d been on vacation and refused to read her emails. I assured her it was not a problem. We'd be delighted to have her come to the show.

"You may not be aware, Miranda, but I graduated Cutler High myself."

"I had no idea."

She chuckled. "I thought not. Before your time. At any rate, I'd love to make a trip back to the old hometown. It'll be fun."

"Sounds great. I'm sure you won't need directions then. I don't know if you'll be staying with family or not but let me know if you need accommodations. We're holding the show at the Armory out on Route 642."

"I know exactly where that is. No problem. And I don't expect to need accommodations, but I'll let you know if that changes. I'm assuming that we'll be setting up on Friday, is that right?"

"Yes, the Quilt Guild members are setting up on Thursday, but we're planning on having some people there all day Friday to help everyone else with their displays. And we'll have frames and tables set up. We'll be displaying several of our own quilts in addition to those for judging and, of course, the heirloom quilts, like yours."

"Sounds good. So I'll see you on Friday afternoon. Oh, wait. One more thing, Miranda. Some of these quilts are quite valuable. Will there be security on site? "

"Of course. We'll have security at the Armory from Friday afternoon through Sunday until everything is torn down and everyone goes home. ROTC students will be patrolling in shifts throughout the weekend, with backup from the Cutler Police Department."

She laughed out loud. "Back in my day that would have been old Sam Johnson. And I think he may have had one part-time officer."

"Well, I'll have you know we have three officers now! Jake Perryman is chief and he has *two* part-timers."

"Are you kidding me? Jake Perryman? He was a little snotty-nosed kid when I was in high school. Imagine, Jake the police chief!"

"Yes, he's doing a great job. His wife's cousin, Judy, is one of our quilters."

"I look forward to meeting everyone. I'll plan on being at the Armory around 3:00 on Friday. Thank you for your help, Miranda."

"See you then."

After we hung up, I checked Marcia out on Google. I learned that she had actually graduated Cutler High back in 1970, which was 10 years ahead of me, and her family name was Hamilton. I wondered if she would have been a student of Harriet or Sarah. I wasn't sure how long they'd been retired but it seems like it's been some time now.

I suddenly realized that Lydia Peterson not responding to our invitation might actually work in our favor. Marcia's would be the oldest antique quilt in the show and that would undoubtedly go a long way to keeping her happy.

Or so I thought at the time, but I've been wrong before.

When I finished, Harry wrapped himself around my legs. He often does that when he's feeling neglected.

“Hello, buddy.” I picked him up and snuggled him for a minute or two. I was itching to tell my news to the other quilters but I’d been running around a good bit lately and it was time for a quiet night with Harry.

“I guess I can wait to tell the girls tomorrow that Marcia is coming.” He gave me a long steady look which I chose to interpret as understanding and approval.

With that, we went into our usual evening routine. I was in my comfy clothes already and it was time for dinner. I filled Harry’s dish and gave him fresh water. Then I filled a plate with leftover beef stew and microwaved it for myself. With that and a glass of wine in my hand, we moved to the living room where I set up my TV tray in front of my chair.

I turned on the news and Harry closed his eyes while he waited for *Jeopardy*. I’d been more than usual so I had a couple of shows recorded, since it’s not on our local channels on Sunday. Harry answers the questions but you have to know him well to be able to tell if he’s right. So we played the game; neither of us knew the Final Jeopardy answer so we called it a draw.

I turned off the TV and picked up the Barbara Freethy novel I’d started a few days ago. I read a lot more when Gabe wasn’t here. *Gabe!* Before I started reading, I commented, “I really miss Gabe, Harry.”

He was lying on his recliner with his head on his paws, but he turned an ear in my direction. Harry likes our routine the way it is and having Gabe in my life has been disruptive, I know. He likes Gabe and lets him have the recliner when he's here, and I'm glad. I don't know if I could spend much time with a man Harry didn't like.

"But he promised to be here next week for the quilt show so that's something."

The ear flicked. Harry's mannerisms and gestures often mirror my first Harry's and one of the many ways they seem most alike is the tendency to communicate as little as possible. It was like learning another language, having to interpret their gestures and body language. That ear flick told me Harry (the cat) was listening to me and sympathized. Anyway, I read to him a bit from my novel until he started to yawn, which made me yawn. So we went to bed.

I closed my eyes but couldn't stop thinking about Gabe. Not just because he was more fun to play *Jeopardy* with than Harry, or because he was much more fun to do some other things with, but because it had been weeks now since we've seen each other. I have no idea where in the world, literally, he might have been, or if he'd been in any kind of danger, on the case that had kept him away these past weeks.

I tried to replay his last visit in my head, how we'd gone to a romantic dinner and come home to enjoy a glass of wine and snuggle. I tried to imagine his strong arms around me as he held me while I slept. I pulled the pillow from the other side of the bed and wrapped my arms around it, taking in that faint scent of aftershave. It was becoming a silly habit—and it was a poor substitute for the real thing.

Seven

I arrived at the library a bit early and prepared a list of the things I wanted to get done by Wednesday. I had scheduled myself off Thursday and Friday to help set up the Armory. As soon as my staff arrived, I called a short meeting.

"You all know about the quilt show this weekend and that I'll be off for a couple of days to help with it. Lucy will be in charge, of course." I smiled at her before I continued. "And I know she can handle anything that might come up, but please know that I'll only be a phone call away."

"The Five Star shipment is coming in on Thursday," William reminded us.

Lucy spoke up. "It's not as big an order as usual so we'll work on it as we have time. If we don't get all the books entered into the system and shelved, we can finish up next week."

William nodded.

Janie added, "And Wednesday morning is the book signing with Andrea Andrews. I expect we'll have a good crowd for her." She blushed, "Her romance novels are pretty popular."

I had to laugh. "Yes, I've seen quite a few of our grandmothers checking them out and hoping no one will notice."

"Isn't that the truth! They're pretty steamy. But honestly, Miranda, we've got this. Like you said, you're still in town in case of a major crisis. And I'm looking forward to coming to the quilt show on Saturday."

"I know you can handle this." I patted Lucy's hand. "And I hope to see all of you at the quilt show. Okay, all done. Anyone have any questions?" After a brief pause, I continued, "Nothing? Then let's unlock those doors." I headed to the breakroom for my coffee before going up to my office.

The morning went quickly and, after lunch, I decided to call the Quilt Shop. Queenie answered on the first ring.

"Queenie's Quilt Shop. Queenie speaking."

"Hi, Queenie, it's Miranda. Are you in the middle of anything?"

"Actually, Harriet and Sarah are here and we're reviewing the judging guidelines. As quilts are entered, we'll assign them to a specific quilt category for judging purposes." She paused. "We even have color-coded cards to place with each quilt, indicating what category it's in. We're almost as organized as Judy and Brittany," she teased.

"Well, I have news to share!"

"Hold on, let me put you on speaker. It's Miranda," she said and I heard a click.

"Hi, everyone. I just couldn't wait to tell you that Marcia Travis is coming!"

There was an odd silence that lasted just long enough for me to hear it.

"That's great news, Miranda!" Queenie replied.

"And get this, her maiden name was Hamilton. She told me she actually graduated from Cutler High."

Harriet spoke up. "I think I remember Marcia. I think I might have had her for Honors English in one of my first years of teaching." She paused again. "I'm glad to hear that she's married and successful now." Period.

Okay, you have to understand that Harriet doesn't talk like that. And she never forgets a student. She always has something personal and warm to say about how lovely or kind or quiet or sweet any former student was, even if she can't say they were particularly bright. Maybe it was just the way she sounded over the phone.

I had no time to dwell on it; I had a list of things to take care of at the Library. Monday picked up speed, as usual, and Tuesday we prepped for our Wednesday signing.

As we expected, it was a circus with our romance author signing and talking for much of the day. She was truly a good sport as her two-hour visit turned to three and then four. By the time we had cleared everyone out and tidied up, we were all exhausted.

Then it was Thursday and the quilt frames and tables were up at the Armory. We were a little surprised by the number of quilters who came to town early to spend a few days with family or to visit with other quilters before the show, making it a mini-vacation as well as a chance to indulge their passion for the work.

The Guild members and a few other locals had already begun hanging their pieces and the hall was filling up with color. The sun streaming in through the windows made rainbows on the floor. We wouldn't normally expose our quilts to sunlight, but the windows were high up and relatively small so a day or two would be okay for most.

My quilt was up and I was proud of it. I'm not the best quilter in the Guild but it appeared to be holding its own with the others so far. The Dresden Plate pattern has been around, as have so many others, for hundreds of years, since they were made out of feed sacks and so on. Petals radiate out from a center circle. Mine had softly rounded edges, which were slightly more floral looking than the completely rounded plates and softer looking than the spiked ones. It was made out of vintage floral fabrics that I'd picked up here and there, with a white background.

Queenie had machine quilted it for me and I gave her full credit on my card in front of its display. Each of the guild's members had membership cards which identified us as such, in case anyone wanted to ask for help with anything local. I was sure we'd have nametags, too, on the day of the show.

Queenie walked up beside me and looked over the quilt. She laid a hand on my shoulder. "You did a nice job, Miranda. Quilts are rarely perfect but it's nice to see the care that goes into them. This quilt reflects your hard work and love for it."

Her words made me warm all over. I turned my head and returned her smile.

I left the Armory in the early afternoon, having enjoyed a chat with Carrie Hilpon, one of our featured quilters, who had arrived from upstate New York. She had brought her sister with her and they were about to walk around the downtown stores so I mentioned that they could stop by Queenie's shop. We didn't have them at the show yet but I did mention they might find discount cards there.

When I got home, Harry was waiting for dinner. It was a little early but he explained in catspeak that his tummy said otherwise. "*Neow, neow!*"

"Fine." I filled his food dish and dumped his water bowl and replaced it with fresh. "But when you're hungry tonight after *Jeopardy*, I don't want to hear it."

He kept eating but his tail swished slightly. I couldn't explain how I knew that meant he heard me but was dismissing something he didn't want to hear, but I got the message.

My phone rang. I have a new ringtone, courtesy of my daughter on her last visit. So it didn't actually ring, it was a voice saying, "RRIINGGG," and the longer I took to answer, the louder and angrier it got. We thought it was funny.

"Miranda Hathaway," I answered formally as I didn't recognize the number.

"Good afternoon. This is Lydia Peterson."

"Oh, wow! Hello, Ms. Peterson." I'm sure my surprise echoed over the line.

She chuckled. "Lydia, please. I'm not a politician. I just heard about your show from a friend and wondered if I might still be able to attend."

"Of course, uh, Lydia, but I sent your invitation weeks ago."

"Really? Well, I'm delighted to hear it but I'm afraid I didn't get it. Perhaps it was lost in the mail."

"I sent it by email."

"Ah, well, that explains it then. I'm compelled to have an email address by my webmaster, but I don't actually use it myself. It's silly, I know, but I prefer to do business in person or by what we are now calling 'snail mail.'"

"I should have followed up with a written invitation. I'm so sorry."

"No harm done. Now, I can be there tomorrow if that works for you." She paused. "Would you want to display the medallion or are your spaces all arranged?"

"Ohmigosh, of course. I just got chills. I can't wait to see it and I'll make sure there's a frame available."

Her laugh echoed. "A woman after my own heart, I see. You know, we found it four years ago and I still get emotional when I look at it. But I do have a frame and set up that I find works well. So I'll bring it along, if that's all right."

"That's fine. Anything we can do to make it easier for you. I'm so delighted, uh, Lydia, that you're coming. We'll all be thrilled to meet you."

"And I you. Shall I make a hotel reservation?"

"No need. I'll take care of it right away."

"Thank you, Miranda. You seem a very efficient person and a kindred quilting spirit. I have a feeling we'll get along just fine."

With that, she was gone and I was so excited I felt like my feet had left the ground. *Wait until I tell the girls!*

I dialed quickly. "Queenie? This is Miranda. Are you still at the Armory?"

"Hi there. Yes, I'm here. And so are Harriet and Sarah. We're just about finished and going to Sylvia's to grab some early dinner."

"Even better. How about I meet you all at Sylvia's in about 15 minutes?"

"You're sounding quite mysterious, Miranda. Is everything okay?"

I decided then to have some fun, so I just said, "See you in a bit," and hung up.

When I turned around, Harry was directly in front of me. I hate that. It's like he's daring me to trip over him. "Harry! What are you doing?"

"*Yeow yeow neow.*" His eyes were narrowed.

"Really? Well, still, be careful, will you? One of these days you're going to kill us both."

A low growl rumbled up out of his throat. That was unusual.

I picked him up as my way of apologizing for scolding him. Then I told him the news. "Guess what? Lydia Peterson is coming and bringing the oldest quilt in Pennsylvania!" He placed his paws against my chest and pushed away so I let him go. "It's a big deal to some of us."

But I was already talking to the tail as he retreated to the living room, and I thought I heard another growl as he jumped up onto his recliner. I had a momentary thought:

Why would Harry not like Lydia Peterson? Then I put it down to his frustration that I was on the run so much these days but that couldn't be helped.

"Well, okay then. See ya later, Harry."

As soon as I walked in and stopped to look around, Sylvia shouted from behind the diner counter, "Last booth on the right, hon!"

"Thanks, Syl. Hi, girls!"

After acknowledging my arrival, all three went silent, looking at me expectantly.

"Well? What's this big news you had to deliver in person?" Queenie's blue eyes were shining.

"Drumroll, please!" I waited but none was forthcoming so I made my own and tapped on the table. "*Brruumm, brrumm, brrumm.*" I continued. "Lydia Peterson just called me. She's coming and she's bringing the medallion!"

While I was disappointed in the drumroll thing, their exclamations of excitement were quite satisfying. Then I noticed Queenie's smile start to fade.

"And Marcia Travis is coming, too?"

"Well, yeah." I watched Harriet and Sarah exchange concerned glances.

After a few tense seconds, Queenie patted my arm. "No big deal. We'll simply arrange the displays so they're as far away from each other as possible."

My bubble started drifting away, not quite bursting but definitely losing altitude.

Harriet added, "This will certainly draw people in, Miranda. You've done a great job."

Sarah nodded her agreement and gave me a weak smile.

Then Queenie spoke in that soothing voice she uses when one of us had royally messed up a quilt and she was going to have to fix it.

"Don't worry about a thing, dear. It will all work out."

Eight

By the time I got home, the bubble had burst. This whole thing could turn out to be an enormous disaster, and it would be my fault for putting these two women in the same room.

When the doorbell rang, I was not smiling—and then I was!

"Hey, beautiful!" Gabe's deep voice was music to my ears.

I threw my arms around his neck, which involved standing on my tiptoes. "I'm so glad to see you."

"Wow, that's good to hear."

He pulled away and then kissed me soundly. We stood there for a few lovely moments, neither of us speaking. I was taking in his scent, listening to his heart beat, and feeling his arms around me. I took a deep breath.

He pulled back and looked down at me. "Now what's upsetting you?"

I gave him a weak smile. "I should probably let you come in first so we can close the door."

"Uh-oh." Nonetheless, he picked up his travel bag and placed it inside on the floor before closing the door. He held onto a tote holding two wine bottles.

I walked into the kitchen with him close behind. Only after we had put together a quick supper did we get back to the cloud over my head.

Between mouthfuls of reheated lasagna which, for some reason, always tastes better as leftovers than it does when first served, I began. "It's been kind of a good news/bad news day. Today, the number one quilter with the oldest quilt in the state called and agreed to come to the show."

"Okay, what's the bad news?"

I sighed, "The number one quilter with the oldest quilt in the state called and agreed to come to the show."

"Is it just me or …" He took a drink of wine.

"Here's the problem. The number two quilter with the second oldest quilt had already agreed to come. It's common knowledge that these two hate each other. It kind of slipped my mind when Lydia, that's number one, called today." I took a bite of warm garlic bread.

"Ouch. Awkward. Do we know why they hate each other?" He had his fork in his lasagna but stopped and looked at me.

"It's kind of a stupid story."

He grinned and reached over to squeeze my hand. "Well, I'm sitting here with you and a glass of wine, so I'm all good. Tell me."

"Here's the short version. Marcia Travis has been showing off her colonial floral quilt for some twenty years or so as the oldest quilt in the state of Pennsylvania. A couple of years ago, Lydia Peterson discovered her family's red medallion quilt, which appears to pre-date Marcia's quilt by about ten years. The dating of these things is, well, not precise."

"Ah, now I get it." He finished his bite and then went on. "When I was a boy, my mother made jams and jellies. Every year she won at least one blue ribbon at the county fair. Her nemesis, I will never forget it, was a woman named Wanda Hickey." I may have snickered just a bit.

"Yeah, I know. Hard to forget. Anyway, they tossed first prize back and forth in several categories and they never spoke. It was life-or-death waiting for the judges to rule at each and every contest."

I waved my fork in his direction. "Exactly."

"Do you think they'll cause a scene?"

"I guess we'll soon see, won't we?" I frowned and took a gulp from my wine glass.

"Think of the draw you'll have—a quilt show with not just amazing and historical quilts but featuring a world wrestling beatdown between Leveler Lydia and Mad Dog Marcia! You won't be able to print tickets fast enough."

I spit out a little wine and grabbed for my napkin. "You are wound up tonight, but thanks for that." I paused. "Harry doesn't like it. When Lydia called today, he read me the riot act."

Gabe's tone was now more subdued. "Well, that can't be good."

Suddenly the cat himself appeared next to Gabe. He reached down a big hand and gave him a manly scratch on his head. Harry looked up at him. I won't go so far as to say "with love in his eyes," but there was at least a male bonding moment of acceptance.

"*Yew, yew,*" Harry said, but it sounded like "you" to his human friend.

I chuckled and Gabe responded, "Yes, it's me. I hope you don't mind my visiting."

Harry yawned and walked away.

Gabe nodded. "I'll interpret that as, 'No, I don't mind.'"

"Works for me." I raised my glass and we toasted with the delicious red wine Gabe had brought down from his collection. I don't remember what it was called, but I do remember that it was very good.

As he travelled the world in his work for the FBI, Gabe purchased wine and shipped it home. He has a fairly significant collection. When he lived in Cutler, he'd rented a small apartment above the local wine shop, The Grapes of Grath, run by a transplanted Californian named Vinnie Grath.

There are a lot of things I like, and am learning to love, about Gabe, and the fact that he takes Harry seriously is one of them. Since his arrival into my life, Harry had shown an uncanny awareness of events outside his little world.

Like when I was kidnapped in Boston last year, Harry went nuts on Diane (my best friend and sometimes cat sitter) and scared her into coming to look for me. Obviously, it all worked out because here I am. Bottom line, Harry seems to have a strong feline antenna and Gabe gets that.

There's also the fact that I know full well my little concerns are nothing compared to matters Gabe has dealt with in the past. But he never belittles them, or me. So Gabe gets Harry and he gets me, and those are pretty good gets as far as I'm concerned.

We watched *Jeopardy* and then we turned in early. When I awoke with Gabe's arm draped over me, I didn't want to move. I turned toward him and snuggled in and went back to sleep. Astonishingly, when I opened my eyes again, he was smiling at me with his amazing crystal blue eyes.

"Hello, you," he said softly.

"Hello yourself," I answered.

What happened next? Maybe we were discussing last night's final *Jeopardy* question? Maybe we were deciding what to have for breakfast? There was a brief interval when Gabe ran to the kitchen and brought us each a cup of coffee. There's nothing better (well, almost nothing) than that first sip. I think we both made the *aaahhh* sound at the same time.

Still, it was after 10:00 when hunger overcame us. We popped out of bed and wandered into the kitchen.

We smiled at each other like a couple of doofy teenagers over toast and scrambled eggs. The urge to lock the door and stay put almost overcame me but—Lydia was coming today!

"Ohmigosh! I almost forgot. Lydia's coming today. I'm meeting her at the Quilt Shop." I checked the clock. "At 1:00." I jumped up and started to clear the dishes. "I have to get a shower and get moving."

"You go ahead. I'll clean this up. I've got some emails to finish and I want to shower, too." Gabe opened his laptop which was lying on the edge of the table. "Is it all right if I meet you later?"

“That would be fine.” But I wasn’t sure I meant it and I suspect my forehead crinkled.

He sighed. “Miranda, I have a couple of quick follow-up reports that I should have sent out to clients yesterday ...” His warm eyes met mine, “… but I wanted to be here.”

What can you say to something like that? “Okay.”

“How about I cook dinner? Or would you rather go out?”

I gave it some thought. “Here’s good.”

A quick shower later, I took off for the Quilt Shop. Harriet, Sarah, and Queenie were already there when I arrived. Queenie mentioned that Judy and Brittany were at the Armory to keep an eye on things until the others arrived. We were chatting excitedly as a red Volvo came to a stop at the curb out front. A white-haired woman removed a box from her back seat and strode toward us.

“There she is!” Sarah spoke first and we all turned toward her. She looked at us and said, “What?”

Just then the door opened. Queenie quickly moved to greet our guest quilter. She brought her over to the cutting table nearest the door.

Lydia placed her box on it. “Hello, everyone. I’m Lydia,” she said with a smile.

I was immediately struck by her resemblance to every image I’ve ever seen of Mrs. Santa Claus: fluffy white hair, twinkly blue eyes, firm smile, and a dimple in her cheek. I liked her immediately.

Then I amused myself with the thought that it did indeed feel like Christmas with all of us gathered around the cutting table as she opened the box containing her quilt.

When she carefully undid the soft sheets from the quilt, folded accordion style, and gently unwrapped part of it so we could see it, there was a moment of reverent silence before excited comments broke out. None of us tried to touch it because we knew better but we did peer closely at the stitching and the technique. It was not just about the age, it was about the skill.

Queenie broke out her magnifying glass and took a really good look at the fabric, thread, and stitching. She nodded her satisfaction and we all breathed a sigh of relief.

Then Lydia, who had put on white gloves, turned it and pulled back a corner to show the initials and a faded date. All I got was "MLP184 (smear)." It was frustrating not to get the last digit.

Lydia explained. "Margaret Litton Peterson was my great-great-great maternal grandmother. I've done some research and, by my estimation, Margaret would have been no more than 25 when she made this quilt."

Her eyes lit up as she explained that she was an only child. "When my cousins, Elsie and Ruth, asked me to help clean out our grandmother's house, we found the quilt! It was tucked away in a trunk in the attic." Her eyes misted. "They were kind enough to let me take it."

Then her face grew somber as she explained that she had no idea it would be the oldest quilt in existence in the state or anywhere else. She had shown the quilt to her own local guild and things took off from there.

Her smile faded. "Then this business with Marcia Travis started. She showed up at my house one day and demanded to examine the quilt herself!" Lydia's hand went to her chest. "I had no idea who she was. Truth is, she was kind of scary. So I asked her to leave." She sighed. "I never intended to create a fuss. I've tried to talk to Marcia since then but she's so upset!"

Everyone nodded. They all looked at me; after all, I was the one who had invited her.

I cleared my throat. "Lydia, as far as we know, Marcia is coming to the show."

She shrugged. "Well, let's look at the bright side. It may give us one more chance to clear the air between us."

Hallelujah!

Nine

It was after 2:00 by the time we got Lydia all set up at the Armory. She said she was going back to the hotel to get some rest so I decided to head home. I needed to be at the Armory early in the morning and I wanted to spend as much time as I could with Gabe. Just as I got into the car, my cell phone started with its obnoxious voice, saying, *RRIINGGG* (must make a note to get that changed—it was funny for a bit but now it was just plain irritating).

When I answered, a familiar voice said, "Remember me?"

I noted just a hint of sarcasm. And her tone clearly indicated that I had been neglecting my best friend. I couldn't really argue with that as we hadn't spoken since I ran into her at Sylvia's a couple of weeks ago.

"Excuse me? Is this someone calling to volunteer to help with the quilt show that's taking place at the Armory *tomorrow*?"

She chuckled. "Okay, okay. So you've been too busy to call your best friend. I get it, but do you have time for a quick drink. I'm buyin'!"

I felt guilty for a second about Gabe alone at my place, but then I knew he was probably busy planning dinner and maybe even had to make a run to the market, so I gave in. I truly had been neglecting my BFF.

"Okay, Tavern, 15."

One of the benefits, if you will, of a long-term friendship is that you can talk in shorthand. She didn't ask me where the Town Tavern was because it was one of our favorite lunch spots. And, normally, we try to have lunch at least once a week, but lately we've both been otherwise occupied for one reason or another.

The waitress also knew our order before we sat down. Lizzie knew everyone, what they drank, what they ate, and probably overheard enough gossip to run her own blog or blackmail half the town. Thank heavens she hasn't done either!

I slid into the booth where an iced tea, unsweetened, waited for me. Diane had lemonade and was stirring it absentmindedly. Sometimes we step it up to alcoholic beverages, but I was already revved up and Diane didn't appear to be in the mood either.

"Hello," I said cheerfully. "Are you sure you're not here to volunteer to help with the quilt show?"

"Uh, no," she said with a smile. "I've done enough volunteering with the school PTO over the years, thank you very much."

"Well, Gabe came down last night, so I have one extra pair of hands anyway, if needed."

"Oooh, extra hands. Do tell." She wiggled her eyebrows at me.

"We're not sixteen anymore, Diane, for heaven's sake."

I took a sip of my tea, picked up a packet of sugar to sprinkle into it, and began stirring it slowly. I know it was a weak attempt at distraction; I could feel the pink flush spread across my cheeks.

She chuckled. "Right. No need. I'll let my imagination run wild."

"You just do that."

She stirred her lemonade some more, but I hadn't seen her take a sip. "I am coming to the show, by the way. Mark has several showings on Saturday so Ethan's coming with me."

"Oh boy. What's he done to deserve that?"

Her eyes widened and she answered in an innocent voice. "Why nothing! I'm just sharing quality time with my son who *is* home for the summer, unlike his older brother who rarely visits and never calls his mother."

"Uh-huh."

"And I may have mentioned that if he didn't come along I expected him to clean out the garage while I was gone."

"Now I understand. So what's up with Devon?"

"He's almost finished his master's so he's started interviewing with several companies. I should be proud and happy for him, but I miss my number-one son." There were tears in her eyes as she finished.

"Sorry, Dee Dee, but it sounds like he's doing well."

"Oh, he's on his way to a wonderful life." She sighed. "I'm not sure I told you, but he has a beautiful girlfriend. I think that's another reason he hasn't been home since Christmas."

"You've been holding out on me. You never said a word."

"Well, you know how college romances are. I figured by the time I told you, they'd be over, but no such luck."

"Diane Murphy, that's a terrible thing to say!"

"I know, and you know I don't mean it. It's just hard to accept that my son is a man and has his own life now and a wonderful future before him that doesn't include me."

I reached across and put my hand over hers. "You know as well as I do that our kids will always need their moms no matter how old they get. Now you have to stop this."

Suddenly, a horrible thought crossed my mind. Was there something going on here that she wasn't telling me?

"Diane, look at me. Is there something else wrong?"

"No. Yes." She sighed. "I think I'm starting 'the change.' Oh God, there I said it out loud. My mood swings are all over the place. I'm laughing one minute and crying the next."

"Well, you know what I went through and I'm glad to be on the other side of that, thank heaven. But my advice is to go to your doctor. *Talk to her*. There are many ways to control all the symptoms."

"Good advice. Now can we please change the subject?"

We both took long sips from our drinks, then Diane spoke up.

"So I heard that Lydia Peterson's in town."

"Yep, and she's really nice, too."

"Nice until she runs into Marcia Travis!" Diane raised an eyebrow.

"How would you know about that? You don't even like quilting!"

"That's not true. I'm still considering making a T-shirt quilt or two for the boys as soon as I can force them to give up the T-shirts. Queenie said she would help me." Her chin lifted. "Anyway, I heard it from Stacy Sheriff, who heard it from Laura Jenkins."

"I guess Laura heard it from one of the other quilters."

She gave me a Cheshire cat grin and her brown curls bounced. "I know something you don't know," she said in the same singsong voice she's been taunting me with since first grade.

In return, I gave her my serious, "Tell me or I'll pull your hair" first-grade look. While she kept her hair relatively short these days, back then her springlike curls were almost irresistible.

She leaned toward me and whispered, "Laura and Marcia are cousins!"

I gasped. "Oh no." Then I felt my shoulders and my spirits sag at the same time. "Laura hates us all. She won't have a good thing to say about the Guild or the show."

"Well, Marcia's staying with her while she's here." She looked at me quizzically. "I'll be kind of surprised if she doesn't put pressure on you guys to show one of Laura's quilts."

I exhaled slowly. "Oh Lord, I hope she doesn't. I don't know what Queenie will do." Then I shrugged. "Well, at least if she takes off in a huff, we'll still have Lydia."

Ten

The bell to Queenie's shop rang merrily but the faces of the women who entered were not happy faces.

"Good afternoon. How can I help you?" Queenie greeted them automatically and then she recognized one of them. She fought to keep her face friendly. "Oh. Hi, Laura. How are you?"

Laura nodded perfunctorily and then smiled slyly. "Queenie, I'd like you to meet my cousin, Marcia."

"Hi, Marcia. Welcome to Cutler."

Marcia managed a small smile. "I have been away for a while." She paused and then met Queenie's eyes. "I was Marcia Hamilton, I'm Marcia Travis now."

Queenie employed an acting mechanism to conceal the fact that she was stunned. She stepped away from the register, lowering her glance to the floor for a moment while she composed her face, and came over to Marcia. "I am so happy to meet you, and I want to thank you for coming to the first Cutler Quilt Show. We're all so excited to see your quilt."

"Yes, well, about that." She squared her shoulders and her voice went stiff. "I understand that you have refused to exhibit several quilts that Laura offered for the show. I'd like an explanation."

Queenie flushed but said quietly, "Have you, uh, seen those quilts?"

"No, I just got into town a couple of hours ago." She glanced at her cousin. "But Laura told me that you don't like her and you let that affect your judgment. That seems very unprofessional to me."

"Well, I suggest you take a look," Queenie replied with increasing confidence. "And maybe you can give Laura some pointers on caring for her quilts." Her chin went up. "I think you will agree with the Quilt Guild that none of them is ready for show. They are in need of serious cleaning and repair." She met Marcia's eyes unflinchingly.

Laura started sputtering and Marcia gave her the "stop" hand. "I will indeed take a look. And then I'll get back to you on whether or not I will be showing the Colonial Floral at your show."

"Thank you. I appreciate that. We will, of course, hold a spot for you."

The women exited the shop with another merry ring and Queenie watched through the window as they argued their way down the street.

She disliked confrontation, for the most part, but now it occurred to her that maybe Marcia could get through to Laura in a way she hadn't been able to so far. Maybe this would be the end of the Laura Jenkins problem. *Sure, and there are no flying monkeys in Oz.*

A short while later, she was mounting a quilt on a frame for the long arm machine, letting the familiar work take her mind off the show for a little while, when the bell over the door tinkled cheerfully.

"Queenie?" I called out.

"Hey, Miranda. Did you get Lydia settled?"

"We did. I know you're dying to see her quilt displayed and it's wonderful. The kids are doing a good job at setting the final frames and at least 20 of the quilts are in place."

Queenie breathed a sigh of relief. "Thank goodness."

"Actually, the reason I stopped by is because you need to know something."

Queenie took one look at my face. "Laura and Marcia are cousins." She said with a grin.

"Too late, huh?"

"They were already here." Queenie shrugged. "We'll have to wait and see."

I knew I had no reason to feel bad but I did. At least, until I got home to the fabulous pasta primavera Gabe was preparing for us.

By the time I'd beaten him at *Jeopardy*, the miserable cousins were gone from my mind. And by the time we'd had a second glass of wine and crawled into bed together, I'd completely forgotten about everything else.

Eleven

The morning of the show dawned bright and clear; it was a good sign, I thought. I showered and dressed quickly, gave Harry his food and morning chat, downed coffee and a muffin, and headed over to the Armory.

Gabe was still sleeping when I left and I let him. He was usually a light sleeper and it made me feel good that he was comfortable enough with me to sleep soundly. I left a note and I'm not telling you what it said.

Feeling ever so slightly guilty about neglecting the library, I made a quick call from the parking lot.

"Hi, Lucy. I'm on my way to the show and checking in to see if everything's okay."

I started talking to voice mail but then Lucy's bubbly voice broke in. "Hey, Miranda. It's all good here. The quilt show is all anyone is talking about!"

"Thanks, Luce. I can't tell you how grateful I am the way you've stepped up while I've been putting in so much time at the Armory."

She chuckled through the phone. "It's been kind of fun, but don't take that to mean I won't be relieved when you're back."

I responded in kind. "I know what you mean. It will be a relief to get things back to normal. This past month has been crazy, but after today it's all over. On the other hand, seeing all the beautiful quilts and getting to talk to the amazing quilters is such a rare opportunity for me and the others."

"Great. You deserve it."

"Thanks. And you're taking a break around lunchtime and coming over, right?"

"I'll be there. I can't wait to see all the quilts."

Judy was at the registration desk with the cashboxes, raffle tickets, sign-in sheets, lots of pens, nametags, all the usual stuff needed to run a show, spread out in front of her. I gave her a wave as I picked up a program and went into the big space to take a look before it got crowded. I checked my watch and saw that I had more than half an hour before the show technically opened.

So I walked up and down the aisles, matching the program entries to the quilts on display. The print shop had done a beautiful job, even adding the last-minute entries for Marcia and Lydia. At the end of the first row, farthest from the doors, was the red medallion. I caught my breath sharply. The full-size quilt mounted on its custom frame was stunning. I paid my respects for a couple of minutes, and then hurried on to look at Marcia's quilt. Queenie told me that a subdued Marcia had called her last night to assure her the quilt would be up by the time the show opened.

And so it was! It was at the very end of aisle four, in the opposite corner from the medallion. The floral colonial was also a beautiful piece of work. Realizing I didn't have much time left to gawk and gasp, I headed back to the front, promising myself a nice, long amble later after the work was done.

Today my task was to sell more raffle tickets. I had picked up the extra tickets and money from shops around town. But we were counting on our walk-in traffic for a big chunk of our sales.

A young man hurried up to me and interrupted my thoughts. "Hello, Mrs. Hathaway. The lady out front asked if you could come help her. Please."

I'd know that red hair anywhere. "It's Jeff Huntley, right?"

He blushed and nodded. "Yeah, Lucy's my sister."

I shook his hand. "Thank you for helping with the setup," I said warmly.

Then I noticed another boy, I guess I should say man, close behind him. This guy was taller, with long black hair hanging down over cold brown eyes. He certainly looked older than Jeff. He smirked at me and made me feel uncomfortable.

"Uh, you're welcome." Jeff sputtered and they moved away quickly, apparently headed toward the cafeteria.

Judy saw me coming and waved me over. "Miranda, can you help me? Brittany's running late."

"No problem. What can I do?" I pulled out a chair and sat down.

"Are you okay with making the nametags before you start selling raffle tickets?"

I nodded. "Sure."

She handed me a list of the presenters and a stack of nametags and I started neatly printing them up. As soon as I finished a stack, I handed them to Harriet who went off to pass them out to the presenters already inside.

Breathless, Brittany ran through the doors, apologizing for being late.

We pulled ourselves together and, when I looked up again, a flood of chattering women and a few men were pouring through the doors.

"Here we go!" Judy said excitedly.

I sold raffle tickets as fast as I could, while Judy and Brittany took admission fees and stamped the hands of the attendees. The noise and general buzzing made the time pass quickly.

Adding to the general confusion, I mean excitement, were the tables from Queenie's Shop. We hadn't originally planned to sell items at the show, but instead of just a display, we had managed to get a couple of extra tables set up, opposite the entrance, with quilting supplies and finished items from the shop. As each person came in, they were greeted by a bright display before they entered the main floor. We even got Queenie to admit later that it added something extra to the show.

A couple of our PTO moms, Sandy and Jessie, were working Queenie's tables. They had told us not to worry; they had rallied the other moms and had relief help coming later. Everything was tagged so it was relatively simple. Both ladies were experienced saleswomen, since they'd been doing bake sales and car washes forever. And they had a vested interest in the new football uniforms and band trip for their kids. They also had Queenie's cell number in case questions came up. She'd be in the building somewhere for the rest of the day. We had a couple of kids handing out her discount cards.

We had each pulled together items from our personal stashes of quilted pillowcases, throw pillows, pot holders, and Christmas items to flesh out the offerings. It looked great and I hoped I'd have some time to shop for myself. Not that I needed anything, but need is such a relative term, right? And it was for a good cause.

The morning flew by, and before I knew it, Queenie and Harriet and Sarah were in front of us, ready to take over for a couple of hours before they did the judging.

I hadn't realized it was noon already, but as I stood up to stretch, Gabe walked in.

"Good morning, ladies. Looks like a great turnout."

Queenie responded before anyone else could. "Good to see you, Gabe. Be sure to check out aisle four. There are several pieces that were quilted on the long arm."

He smiled at her. "Thank you. I'll do that. First, though, I'm hoping to steal this lovely lady for lunch." He looked at me.

Sarah answered quickly, surprising us yet again. "You kids go ahead. We got this covered!"

Harriet and Queenie shared a quick smile before Harriet confirmed it. "Sure, go. We've got this!"

I walked around the table and Gabe took hold of my hand. We walked back aisle four together. Gabe smiled down at me, his wonderful blue eyes crinkling. “Let’s take a quick look at these quilts and then get something to eat.”

“Great. I’m starving.”

So, after we admired the machine-quilted items in aisle four, and gave Queenie a nod and thumbs up on the way out, we headed to the parking lot.

“I thought we’d get away for a few minutes. Are there any restaurants nearby?”

I blew out a breath. “I sure could use a break from the crowd. Billy’s BBQ is about a mile up the road and I haven’t been there in a while.”

“Well, I’ve never been, so let’s go!”

In no time, we were inhaling pulled pork barbecue sandwiches.

Billy’s is a local institution. It serves pork and beef barbecue on a Kaiser roll and that’s pretty much it. You got your cardboard tray with one of the two sandwiches, a bag of chips, and a bottle of soda or water. *Period.* But, oh my, it was so good. You could tell by the number of times you had to wipe your face to keep the juice from running down your chin.

“I’d almost forgotten how good these sandwiches are. Do you like it?”

Gabe was eating in silent concentration. I knew he was trying hard not to dribble. He wiped his chin. “It’s amazing. I can’t believe we’ve never been here before. This barbecue sauce is the best I’ve ever tasted and I’m not kidding. Billy could bottle this stuff and make a fortune.”

"Yeah, well, I don't see that happening. Like many places around here, this is a family-owned and -operated business. They're open year-round and do everything right here. So sometimes they stick a sign on the door and go away for a couple of weeks."

"So now, tell me the truth. How's the show going? It looked like there are lots of people coming through," Gabe asked as he wiped his chin again.

I swallowed a mouthful myself before answering. "I have no idea how much money we've taken in but there's been a steady stream of people ever since we opened and you saw the parking lot. We have some of the ROTC kids supervising the parking in order to fit them all in. I've sold a lot of raffle tickets. I'm so glad James gave me 2,000. We've been taking turns with quick breaks here and there but it's been pretty nonstop. So I think we'll be glad when it's 4:00 but it's been a wonderful experience so far."

"Any smackdowns between the Leveler and Mad Dog?"

I choked on a bit of pork and had to take a drink of water. "Not that I've heard about. We put them in opposite corners of the space. I expect there are so many people between them that they can hardly see each other."

"That's disappointing, in a twisted kind of way," he said quietly, but with a sly grin.

I threw a crumpled napkin at him. "Maybe for you. But we're not trying to clear the place out just yet, so quiet is good."

We drove back in companionable silence, lost in our thoughts and our full bellies. Gabe pulled into the parking lot along the side where the workers were parking. “So you’re staying till 4:00, then?” He looked at his watch.

“Well, to be realistic, it will likely be 4:00 or even a bit after until we actually get the doors closed. I hope we don’t have to take down all the quilts after that but I don’t really know.”

“Okay. Well, I think I’ll head out for now and come back around 4:00, that way I’ll be here in time to help with any heavy lifting.”

I squeezed his hand in gratitude. “Thank you.”

He leaned over and kissed me gently. I responded enthusiastically and it started to get a little warm in the car.

When we separated, I said, “I’ll see you later and we can continue this ‘discussion’ then.”

“Sounds good to me. Maybe we’ll catch dinner out somewhere before we go home to continue this ‘discussion’ even further.”

He knew me so well. I was stuffed to the gills now but I never miss a meal.

As I walked toward the Armory, I stopped and turned around. He was still there, watching, and he waved. I gave a small wave back as I went through the doors.

It had taken some getting used to, having a man in my life again. I was young when I met Harry and we dated for several years before we got married. I never even considered having to get to know another man.

I hadn’t been looking when I found Gabe, who was turning out to be as wonderful as my Harry had been. I was one lucky woman and I knew it.

Gabe watched her walk away. One of the most beautiful things about Miranda was that she didn't know how beautiful she was. And it was natural beauty. She looked as good when she woke up in the morning as she did when they dressed to go out to dinner.

Not one of the women he'd dated since the divorce had the depth of Miranda. Spending time with her was never a chore and never boring.

"I'm one lucky bastard!" he muttered to himself as he watched her go through the doors.

Twelve

When I got back, the faces behind the front tables were intense but happy. I asked if I could relieve someone. Harriet pointed over to the shop tables where only one woman was working and asked if I could help out. She also had a message for me. "Lucy stopped by. Said to tell you the show is fabulous. She's thinking of taking up quilting! And she'll talk to you later."

"I'm sorry I missed her." I laughed. "Knowing Lucy, it will be quilting for about a week before she moves on. I think she's started crocheting and knitting already this year!" I headed over to the shop tables. Becky Anderson was bagging a pillow for a customer. When the lady left, I spoke. "Hey there, Becky, how's it going?"

"Hi, Miranda. Great! At this rate we may sell out before the show closes. Isn't it wonderful! I was so excited when Sandy called me and asked if I could volunteer some time today. I can't begin to thank you all for doing this for the school."

"We're really excited about it. The way it looks, we should be able to reach our goal."

"As you know, the PTO is always having bake sales and car washes, but this is incredible." She started helping a woman looking through charm packs of fabric while I sold some Christmas potholders to another. When our happy customers left clutching bags, she leaned over and said, "Jenny Sorensen called to say she's running late, but should be here any minute."

"No worries. I'm happy to help any way I can." Then we got busy again. A few minutes later, when Jenny showed up, I returned to my raffle ticket sales.

The tickets were still going strong and several people had come back to buy more after seeing the Husqvarna, which was on display by the shop tables. With each sale, I could feel my chances shrinking. I forced myself to consider all the money we were making for the school. But don't get me wrong, I still wanted to win!

With Judy, Brit and I back at the tables, Queenie and the twins were free to take a break and do the judging. Sarah and Harriet went to the cafeteria for a quick tea break. But Queenie felt compelled to take a walk around the show. She headed down the center aisle, automatically looking to the left and right. Marcia Travis was on her left and Lydia Peterson on her right. Or that's how it should have been—except Marcia was standing in front of Lydia, shaking a finger in her face.

A hush had fallen over the area around them, quilters and visitors frozen and listening with concern.

Queenie hurried over.

"Don't even try to tell me you just happened to come across a quilt older than mine, you, you, faker!" Marcia hissed.

Lydia puffed up. "How dare you?"

Queenie stepped in between them. "Ladies, this is a public forum." She turned. "This behavior is unacceptable, Marcia. Go back to your quilt now."

Jake Perryman, in uniform, appeared beside her. He gave Marcia his official look. She huffed and stomped away.

"Should never have invited that one," he murmured to Queenie. "Bad attitude."

She sighed. "I know."

Lydia took a deep breath. "I'm sorry, Queenie. It's hard not to rise to the bait."

Queenie nodded. "I understand and I apologize. It's a shame when quilters don't have the sensibilities that they should."

Lydia managed a smile. "I think the problem is that we're not quilters in the sense you are. Marcia and I had relatives who were but I do only a little quilting and I'm not sure she does any. Every quilter I've encountered has a kind heart and a giving spirit that we can only try to emulate." She touched a cross on a chain around her neck. "But sometimes it's about being a Christian, good old common courtesy, and respect, too."

Queenie nodded. "Amen."

Queenie went off to find the twins and finalize the judging. Jake continued to amble around the hall, chatting here and there, but always keeping an eye on Marcia.

The time seemed to be speeding by. Queenie came out to let us know once the judging was complete. She sat down next to me, relieving Brittany.

I leaned over, "Any problems?"

She smiled wearily. "I broke them up a while ago. Marcia can't seem to stay put or keep her opinions to herself. Jake popped in and is walking around awhile. I'm hoping the sight of the uniform might shut her down. I don't doubt that she'll be back to telling everyone that Lydia's quilt is a fake as soon as he leaves."

"That's awful. No signs of a thaw, then?"

She shook her head.

I shrugged. "Well, at least there's been no bloodshed. Not much you can work with there. I like Lydia and I can't imagine there's any way she would fake an antique quilt."

"It's not easy to do either. It would take a great deal of research on the fabric, dyes, and threads. If she's not making money out of it, what would be the point?"

I nodded. "Exactly. By the way, Gabe is coming back in case we need extra muscle to help close up."

Queenie's eyes warmed. "I'm glad."

I knew that those two words covered a lot more than his physical presence at the show and nodded my understanding. We turned our attention to the cashboxes in front of us.

As the show wound down, we were able to take turns peeking into the hall. Ribbons were on view at the prize quilts. A few quilters started to remove their pieces but most were busy chatting. I couldn't wait to walk through and check the quilts out more carefully.

Brittany returned from her coffee break to report that, now that lunch was over, the quilters were taking advantage of the cafeteria space to swap stories, share tips, and show pictures of their grandkids and their quilts. We could hear the laughter and excited buzz and it made us all smile.

But we did heave a collective sigh of relief when Queenie made the announcement over the PA system that the show would close in 10 minutes and thanked everyone for coming.

True to his word and punctual as usual, Gabe came through the door, fighting the tide of people going out. I closed my cashbox, placed it under the table, and took him to the cafeteria for a quick cup of coffee before we viewed the quilts. Sarah and Harriet joined us. The usually quiet and shy twins were all smiles as they were greeted by some of those making their way out of the cafeteria.

We heard Queenie announce the closing over the loudspeaker. "Ladies and gentlemen, it is now 4:00. The first Cutler Quilt Show is closed. We congratulate our winners and express our gratitude to everyone who displayed today. We also thank you for your support of this event, as all proceeds will go to the Cutler High School for extracurricular activities. The winner of the Husqvarna quilting machine will be notified within the next 24 hours. Happy Quilting and have a great weekend!"

Jake tipped his hat on the way out the door and we gave him a nod and a couple of thumbs-up.

Leaving Sarah and Harriet to chat with the remaining quilters, Gabe and I got up and went over to the wide double doors, propped open to each side. As we started our walk down the first aisle, Gabe commented on the quilts almost as much as I did.

When he had wandered into Queenie's over a year ago and joined the Guild, we'd discovered that his now ex-wife had gotten herself a 12-foot long arm quilting machine and, in an effort to find something they could do together, Gabe read the manual and learned how to operate it. She did the tops and basted them together and then he quilted them. Sadly, it didn't save their marriage, but for those of us who didn't want to go near the darn thing, he was a godsend.

I was happy to machine quilt smaller projects on my sewing machine and Sarah and Harriet are amazing hand quilters, but it was Gabe and Queenie on the long arm who were speedy enough to keep our projects flowing.

I appreciated the perfection of the machine patterns and the ability to finish pieces faster than at home but, in my heart, I had a special place for the hand-quilted pieces. I kept that to myself today.

The grand prize and blue ribbon had gone to Amy Truehorn's bargello and she was delighted. This was the first time she'd shown it, but I'm sure it won't be the last. It's a wavy helix, and a masterpiece of tiny blue, green, and gold squares. I keep promising myself I'll try a bargello one of these days but I'm not sure I have the discipline or the eyesight.

Second place, to my delight, had gone to a black-on-white hand-quilted whole cloth quilt. This type of quilt consists of a single piece of fabric with a generally complex overall pattern, usually in a contrasting thread. It takes a lot of planning and self-confidence. With a variety of quilting stitches circling out from a center star, this one was a stunner.

Third place was a traditional log cabin, all hand-pieced and tied. Tying quilts is an old-school method wherein you take something like a light yarn or crochet thread, something more durable and stronger than sewing thread, and simply tie the three layers of the quilt together at regular intervals. It added an authenticity to the mix of colorful scraps of fabric.

It brought to mind how the true roots of quilting were meant to use up small pieces of fabric and provide bedding and clothing when larger pieces were hard to come by. I smiled at it, believing that Harriet and Sarah's influence was especially behind this choice. I agreed with all three choices.

Queenie had even managed to come up with a historically significant category so that the medallion and colonial floral both received gold ribbons of recognition.

We walked down the aisle and stopped by the medallion. Gabe was seeing it for the first time and he took a few minutes to peer at it closely in silent awe. He read the card that Lydia had produced with the few facts as she knew them. I stayed quiet until he straightened up and shook his head before turning to me with a smile.

"This piece makes machine quilting feel like cheating."

I chuckled. "I always feel like that, I admit, although there's no part of quilting that doesn't require skill, patience, and love."

He squeezed my hand and we turned to the quilts on the other side of the aisle. It made me smile as I watched and realized that Gabe was taking in the less artistic, more tactical, aspects of the big hall. His eyes flicked to the exits, lighting, and emergency systems when he thought I wasn't looking. I'd noticed this before any time we went to a restaurant or any new place, for that matter. Once FBI, always FBI!

When he excused himself to go to the men's room, it often took a while. I finally figured out he was sort of "casing the joint," making sure we had ways out. It was a little weird at first but I had to admit I always felt safe with Gabe. If there was a problem, he would fix it. If there was danger, he would fight it or find a way to save me from it. I had no doubt.

We made it to the corner where Marcia's quilt had been and I was surprised to find it gone. She had apparently cleared out right after the show closed. We had left Lydia in the cafeteria, holding court with some others, answering questions about her quilt. I figured Marcia couldn't deal with her getting all that attention. It truly was a shame that these two women with so much in common couldn't reach a truce.

Thirteen

As we walked down the last aisle of quilts, my mind kept wandering down that sorry path. Quilters are inherently caretakers and good people. Marcia had no business saying mean things about Lydia's quilt. It simply went against the grain. I had to admit I was glad Marcia was gone.

Suddenly, I heard a *whoosh* sound and it started raining. Raining? I looked up. *Ohmigod.* The sprinklers were on. Before I could say a word, Gabe went running.

I heard screams and then Queenie came racing through the door from the cafeteria. One of the Tech School boys threw open a closet door and there was a pile of big blue tarps inside. She ran over and grabbed an armload.

"The medallion!" she gasped and raced away.

I was right behind her. We hastily threw tarps over tables of folded quilts as we went. Then we each grabbed the edge of a tarp and threw it up and over the frame where the medallion hung, starting to sag already. I wanted to cry but didn't have time.

I passed another boy on his way into the hall with an armload of blue tarps. I screamed at him and pointed. "Cover the quilts on the tables."

He nodded and took off for the other side of the room.

Lydia Peterson came running toward us, her face as white as her hair. Her mouth opened like she was trying to speak but nothing came out.

Then it stopped. We all stood still for a moment. Gabe came quickly to my side.

"You, you …," I sputtered.

He put an arm around me. "… found the water shutoff valve."

I looked at Queenie, her eye makeup running down her face and her always poufy hair squished flat. I probably looked like a drowned rat myself. I looked around the hall at the drooping quilts and the puddles on the floor.

There was still no time to cry.

By now half a dozen people huddled around the medallion, with Lydia in the middle of them. I could hear her sobbing as we approached. Tears were in my own eyes and I saw stricken faces all around.

We all helped get the heavy, sopping wet quilt down from the frame and Queenie, still wet and unusually pale, having wiped her face on the bottom of her tunic, bent over the wet fabric.

"Towels! Dry towels!" she shouted. Our eyes met and I nodded.

Shower room. I had passed the sign down the hall near the restrooms. I took off down the aisle. As usual, Gabe was a step ahead of me and making better time with his longer legs. I didn't have time to wonder how he knew where we were going. I passed Sarah and Harriet helping to take down some other quilts and pointed them toward the medallion.

When I got to the shower room, Gabe handed me an armload of oversized white towels. Then he picked up his own load and waited.

"Go!" I yelled. "I'm okay. Go!"

He took off running and I followed at the best pace I could muster. As I hustled up the aisle, I heard Queenie issuing orders. By the time I got there, Sarah, Harriet, Lydia, Gabe, and Queenie had each grasped an edge of the quilt and lifted it, each stretching an arm under to support the middle. I wedged in along the side to help. We moved slowly, as one unit, out of the wet floor space and into the front entry, which was dry. On orders, Gabe and I let go and spread a layer of towels on the floor. The quilt was gently laid down on the towels.

Then Queenie ordered another layer of towels to be placed on top of it. She spoke quietly to Lydia who joined her on her knees; together they began to roll it up, sausage-style, pressing gently.

When they reached the end of the quilt, they stood. Queenie asked Gabe to pick it up and put it into her car. She thanked us all and asked that we stay around to help with the other quilts as long as we could. Everyone nodded. She whipped out her phone and called Fred Morrison, our local dry cleaner.

Then she and Lydia took off to his shop where I was praying he would have the expertise to gently dry the quilt.

I was waiting for Gabe at the doors. We looked at each other and then walked slowly back into the Armory hall. There were more than a dozen quilts still being taken down and folded up by their owners. There was an eerie silence, except for the dripping.

When the kids from the high school and Tech School got there, Gabe and I explained what had happened and asked them to help mop up before they began tearing down the tables and the frames that had been emptied.

We went up and down each aisle, doing what we could. Violet Hempsfield, owner of the second-prize whole cloth quilt, was actually comforting her neighbor as she helped fold a damp hexagon quilt. She managed a smile as I approached and asked about her quilt.

"Don't worry, honey. I prewashed it and had just placed it in the case when those sprinklers went off." She pointed to a storage case. "All tucked in, safe and sound."

"I'm so glad." I remembered the bargello and looked around anxiously. "Have you seen Amy's bargello?"

"The first prize winner, right?" Her face fell. "I heard her wailing a minute ago. She seems pretty upset."

"I'd better go over there."

"Better you than me, honey."

Amy's quilt was down but sopping wet. She was alternating between sobbing over her work as she folded it up into a heavy square and angrily asking who had done this awful thing. There wasn't much I could do about either. I offered to drive her to the dry cleaner to see if he could help.

She shook her head. "I just want to go home. I am never coming back here again. This is unconscionable! How could you people let this happen?" She tossed her ribbon on the floor, slammed the lid on her case, and stalked off.

If I thought I couldn't feel any worse after seeing Lydia's quilt, I was wrong. Still, there was no time to cry. There were other soggy quilts and other quilters to comfort.

Harriet and Sarah, who lived closest, ran home to change. Sarah brought back an outfit for me because we're close to the same size. Gabe, my always prepared guy, had a go-bag in the trunk of his car, of course. So we were able to dry off and keep going.

For another hour or so, Harriet, Sarah, Gabe, and I kept going, providing towels and helping other quilters pack up their quilts and head out. Most of them would be fine with a gentle drying and reshaping. Only the fragile antiques were truly threatened by water.

Then the rumors started. Gabe and I overheard another quilter comment on the fact that Marcia and her colonial floral had been gone before the sprinklers started. How fortuitous! Indeed!

At that point, we sent the exhausted twins home. Helping out the overwhelmed teens, Gabe pitched in with the teardown and I mopped up water puddles. Another hour passed before we saw the kids out and turned off the lights. On our way out, I glanced at the front tables. The cashboxes were gone and I admired Queenie for remembering to see to them in the midst of the chaos.

I called her from the car. "Hi, Queenie. It's Miranda."

"How'd you make out?" she asked.

"About as you'd expect. The newer pieces will be fine after they're dried. It's mostly Lydia's piece everyone was worried about. Amy Truehorn took it badly. Her bargello was dripping. But she wouldn't let us help her."

"What happened to Marcia's?"

"Marcia had left before the sprinklers came on," I answered quietly, having no energy left and no heart to sound accusing.

"Oh, really?"

I sighed. "Yeah, that was pretty much the reaction of the others. I'm afraid the rumors are starting already."

"I'm sure." She sounded unusually disheartened. "On the good news side, we seem to have done all right with the medallion. We're letting it finish drying overnight and then Lydia should be able to wrap it up and take it home." Queenie sighed this time. "She is so lovely, Miranda. Once she saw how Fred was caring for it, she actually said it looks better now that it has been cleaned!"

"Wow."

"I know. So let's get some rest and we'll talk tomorrow."

"Sounds good. The Armory's locked up safe and sound."

I hung up and Gabe and I made the rest of the trip in silence.

When we got home, Harry met us at the door. He took a look at both of us and retreated to his recliner. I couldn't blame him. Always aware of my duties as cat staff, though, I filled his food and water dishes and he appeared for dinner. I stroked his velvet head.

"Tough day, Harry," I said sadly.

"*Eoowww,*" he acknowledged with a glance at his dish.

"Go ahead and eat, Harry."

He ambled over to his dish and started crunching.

I admired his life-goes-on philosophy; I was starving but my first priority was a hot shower. It certainly didn't feel like the time to share one so Gabe and I went to separate bathrooms and came back refreshed and warmed.

I hung my own poor damp Dresden Plate quilt on the line in the back yard. It was warm enough to dry it out naturally. I hadn't checked a forecast but as I walked back into the kitchen, Gabe looked up from the not-so-celebratory dinner he was fixing.

"It's not going to rain," he said matter of factly.

"Thanks." I managed a smile as he had anticipated my concern.

I was still coming to terms with how our lovely, exciting show had ended. And I have to admit that the combination of the work over the last month and the disaster today had left me physically and mentally drained.

Needless to say, dinner was a subdued affair. We managed to pull together a decent meal, but we left the wine in the refrigerator.

We were sharing a piece of cheesecake that I had found in the freezer and thawed while we ate, along with a cup of fresh coffee, when my house phone rang. I decided not to answer it. I wasn't interested in rumors or commiseration at this point. Then I heard Zoey's voice on the machine.

Seeing the look on my face, Gabe stepped over and picked it up. In a low voice, I heard him responding to her questions. No doubt she wanted to hear how the show had gone. Frankly, I was glad she wasn't here.

After a few minutes he came back to the table and stopped to rub my shoulders ever so gently. "She'll talk to you later."

"Thanks." I smiled at him. "And in case no one has said it, you were wonderful today."

He smiled back. "So were you."

"You knew where the shutoff valves were?"

He shrugged. "Old habits."

I laid my hand over his. "Remind me never to complain again about you wandering off to look a place over."

He picked up my hand and kissed it. Then he frowned. "I hate having to say this to you, Miranda, but I believe that this was deliberate. There was no smoke, no fire, nothing to set the sprinklers off."

I gasped. "Oh no! Who would do such a thing?" My brain kicked into gear and automatically started a list. "Marcia? Or maybe Laura?

"Ordinarily, as an investigator, I would ask who stood to benefit from the crime. In this case, I wonder if there was no benefit other than revenge or spite. If it was simply about ruining Lydia's quilt, the needle certainly points to one of those two. As I understand it, only the antique pieces were vulnerable?"

I nodded. "I think that's right. Modern fabrics and threads are stronger and many quilters actually prewash their fabrics."

Gabe took a drink of his coffee. "Well, I suggest we sleep on it. Maybe the first question to ask is, 'Are you sure you really want to know?'"

Out of nowhere, Harry had appeared. "*Neowww.*"

We both laughed and I raised a coffee cup to him. "I understand what you're saying, Harry, but I don't think it's going to be quite that simple."

Fourteen

When we climbed into bed and Gabe pulled me into his arms, it was finally time to cry. All the tears I'd held in for hours poured out. Once they started, I couldn't stop. Gabe didn't say a word. He gently stroked my hair while I soaked his t-shirt. All the emotions I'd pushed back all day spilled out.

The thought that someone had purposely sabbatoged our wonderful show was beyond my comprehension. All our hard work to pull off this benefit for the school! All those beautiful quilts callously drowned. I could still hear Lydia crying and Amy so angry.

When my tears subsided and I could hear Gabe's steady heart beat in my ear, I slipped out of bed and into the bathroom. I washed my face and closed my eyes for aminute. When I looked in the mirror, I saw a determined woman looking back at me. They weren't going to get away with it, no matter what Harry thought. We were going to get to the bottom on this. I took a deep breath.

Gabe had changed his shirt and was waiting for me. He kissed my forehead gently.

"Are you okay?"

"Absolutely. Better than okay."

"You know we'll figure this out, right?"

"Damn right!" I kissed him soundly. I turned on my side, as I always do, and he threw one arm over me, as he always does. It's not exactly sleeping in his arms, but its close enough.

To my surprise, I didn't dream about soggy quilts.

For the second day in a row, I woke up first. I slipped out of bed and turned on the coffee. Harry waited patiently (more or less) for his breakfast. He was very quiet this morning but it felt like that kind of a day. Hopefully, we could have a quiet Sunday to recover from the trauma of yesterday. I was sitting by the window watching the birds outside having their breakfasts when Gabe came out, rubbing his eyes.

"Good morning."

He croaked, "Coffee."

I pointed to the pot. "You're all set. Help yourself."

"Bless you."

He poured himself a cup, popped some bread into the toaster, and then sat down across from me. After downing half his cup, he was able to speak. "So what would you like to do today?"

I shrugged. "As little as possible?"

On cue, the phone rang.

He laughed out loud. "I'm guessing that's not going to happen."

I glanced at the clock. Eight o'clock on Sunday. Really? I let it go to the machine. Then I heard Queenie's voice and picked up the phone in the middle of her message.

"Hi, Queenie."

"I'm sorry to call so early."

"Well, I'm still having my first cup of coffee and, honestly, I wouldn't have picked up for just anybody."

She chuckled. "Thanks for picking up then. I was wondering if you might be able to come back to the Armory with me today to make sure everything's in order. Our cashboxes are still there and I won't feel comfortable until I get them back."

I swallowed. *Oh dear.* "Sure. How soon?"

"Is an hour okay? I have to shower and eat something myself."

"Fine. Would it be okay if Gabe came with me?"

"Absolutely. I never mind having a man around."

I returned to the table where Gabe was buttering our toast. He handed me a slice. "Still relaxing today?"

"Very funny." I frowned. "Gabe, Queenie said the cash boxes are still in the Armory."

He gave me a worried look. "I didn't see them. Did you?"

"No."

"Damn."

I sighed and cast a glance to heaven. "Oh, please."

We got to the Armory right on time and Queenie pulled in beside us. I handed her the keys. She found the switch and light flooded the huge space. The tables were still sitting where we had left them. The cashboxes were on the floor beneath the chairs. No wonder Gabe and I hadn't seen them.

I breathed a sigh of relief—too soon.

Queenie raced over and grabbed the first one. "Oh no! Oh no!" She sank into a chair and buried her face in her hands. I picked up the raffle ticket box: too light and also empty. Tears came to my eyes.

I raised my stricken face to Gabe. He blew his breath out slowly. "I think it's time to call the police."

I flopped into a chair beside Queenie and offered her a tissue. She squared her shoulders and nodded. "Dammit." She glanced my way. "Sorry, but damn, damn, damn!" She took a deep breath and struggled to compose herself. We let her have that moment in silence.

Her voice was shaky. "Gabe, will you make the call while Miranda and I do a quick walk-through?"

He nodded. "No problem. And I'm truly sorry, Queenie."

She raised her hand to stop him. "I have to thank God that we took some of the money out at lunchtime and gave it to the booster moms. So we haven't lost everything." She cleared her throat and stood up. "Right now, we owe it to the mayor and the ROTC to make sure we give this place back the way we got it." She marched into the big hall and I followed meekly. I admired her spirit; I don't know when I've felt so … defeated.

"Colonel Halston asked me to leave the additional lighting. He thought it might come in useful," Queenie said softly.

"Good," I answered firmly. Without thinking, I added, "This floor is certainly the cleanest it's ever been!"

She looked at me and her mouth started to turn up at the corners. I realized what I had said and suddenly it struck me as funny. I started to laugh and she joined me. When Gabe came in we were laughing hysterically.

"Uh, are you ladies okay?" he asked in his deep voice.

I have no idea why that set us off again but it did and he grinned down at us. "The Chief is on his way."

We finally wiped our eyes and answered him. "We're fine." I put my arms around Queenie's shoulders. "We're going to be just fine."

She patted my hand and we finished our round of the Armory. With the exception of a few random pieces of trash and a couple of plastic cups, everything looked good. The only thing left to do really was remove the tables from the entrance hall. They belonged to the Armory so we tore them down and stacked them against the wall.

"Hey." I glanced at my watch. "How about we treat you to brunch at the Hillside? Someplace special to put this out of your mind for a while."

She smiled. "Thanks, hon, but I need to wait here for Jake to file a report, then catch up on everything at the shop and finish up some paperwork." She paused. "At least we gave out the cash prizes yesterday before this happened."

"We can wait here with you."

"No. Not necessary. You two go have a nice brunch and try to relax. I can handle this." She pulled up a chair and sat down next to the empty cashboxes.

Feeling only slightly guilty, Gabe and I drove to the Hillside Inn. As we entered the charming dining room with its view of the surrounding countryside, I felt my spirits start to lift. We had both turned off our phones and that helped.

Over dessert, I cleared my throat and Gabe looked up expectantly.

"Thank you, for everything."

Gabe's puzzled look was replaced by suspicion. "Am I going somewhere?"

I chuckled. "No, I just want to make sure you know that I'm not taking you for granted."

Relief flooded his face. "Of course you're not. It's been a tough couple of days for everyone."

"I know. And I realize that when you decided to come down for the weekend, this may not have been what you had in mind."

He squeezed my hand and then threw a wave around at the lovely restaurant. "Well, this is exactly what I had in mind."

We went home to peace and quiet. Harry greeted us with a demand for attention and, after being petted and engaged in conversation for a few minutes, he disappeared, no doubt for a nap to recover from the exertion.

"I think we could use a nap." I smiled and stood on my tiptoes to put my arms around Gabe's neck.

We retreated to my room. We didn't turn our phones back on until midafternoon. I had a call from Jake Perryman asking if he could stop by. The calm relaxation and warmth I felt from being with Gabe started to wane.

Then it hit me like a ton of bricks. This theft would be the biggest thing to hit Cutler since, well, our pursuit of the "Quilt Ripper" last year. And poor Jake had missed out on that. He'd be all over this stolen money like it was the most exciting thing to happen during his tenure as chief. And it might well be! I sighed at the thought of a lengthy police interrogation.

Jake was a big man whose consistently red face worried me every time I saw him and today was no exception. When he rang the doorbell, Gabe answered it and led Jake back to the kitchen where I had just made a fresh pot of coffee.

"Hey, Miranda."

"Take a load off, Jake. Can I get you a cup of coffee?"

"No, thanks. I'm good." He wedged himself into a kitchen chair and we took our own seats opposite him. "Let's get this over with, okay?"

He was clearly embarrassed and I softened a bit. "Sure."

"Right." He dug out his notebook and pen. "So yesterday there was a quilt show at the Armory, lots of traffic in and out."

We nodded.

"Right. Then around 4:30, after the show was closed to the public, the sprinklers came on. Is that what you remember?"

Lord, had he never heard of leading the witness? I glanced at Gabe, who was struggling to keep a straight face.

"Yes." I decided to move this along. "There was a mad rush to get the quilts out of the water, as you may imagine. Once the sprinklers were turned off, Queenie and Lydia

Peterson, the owner of one of the two antique quilts that was being shown, went to Fred's to try to salvage her quilt."

He nodded. "Do you have any idea how the sprinklers came on?"

Gabe cleared his throat and I let him run with the answer to that. "No idea. The water shutoffs are in a hallway next to the main room. I ran out there and shut them off."

Jake sighed. "But for the sprinklers to come on in the first place there would have to be smoke or fire. Did you see any such smoke or fire?"

"No, nothing."

"So they'd have to be deliberately triggered."

"Yes."

Part of Jake had clearly been hoping for an accident or a malfunction. No such luck!

He glanced at Gabe. "And how did you know where the shutoff valves were?"

The surprise must have shown on my face. It was a good question.

Gabe smiled. "Jake, you know I'm retired FBI and now I work as a private investigator. I scope out any building I'm in, it's automatic. While the show was winding down, I took a walk around the corridors surrounding the show area." He shrugged. "Just a habit."

"I see. So, moving on, most of the people had left after 4:00. What were you doing then?" He looked at me.

"Gabe and I took advantage of the chance to walk around the exhibits before they were all taken down. Queenie had told all the guild members who were working the show that they'd have a chance to see the quilts at the end of the day."

"So all the guild members stayed after the show was over?"

"No. Brittany and Judy wanted to get home so they left as soon as the doors were closed to the public."

"Right. Where were you, exactly, when the sprinklers came on?"

"We were in the last row of tables, probably about halfway down. We were almost finished looking at the displays."

He glanced at his notes. "You indicated that there were two antique quilts. Yet you didn't mention a rush to save the second one."

He surprised me again. I hesitated and Gabe gently gave me an elbow. "It wasn't there."

"The owner had already left," Jake said flatly.

"It seems so."

"Are you aware of any relationship between the owners of the two antique quilts?"

I cleared my throat, trying to focus on facts, not hearsay. "Lydia Peterson, owner of the quilt that was there at the time, had expressed to me her dismay over some resentment on the part of Marcia Travis, owner of the second quilt."

He nodded. "And do you know the source of these feelings?"

"Until Lydia found her quilt a few years back, Marcia's had been known as the oldest quilt in Pennsylvania. She took it hard being relegated to number two."

"Okay. Now, at the end of the day, after the water was off and almost everyone had left, you two stayed."

Gabe nodded. "We helped the crew of kids from the Tech School clean up and then locked up when we were done. Obviously, Queenie would have been in charge but she was at the dry cleaner's with the damaged quilt."

I added, "And we sent Harriet and Sarah home because they were both clearly exhausted."

Jake made a few more notes. "So, as far as you know, you were the last ones out the door."

We looked at each other and I remembered a sentence from my legal shows. "To the best of our knowledge."

He coughed. "Did you happen to see the cashboxes on your way out?"

"No."

"Yet they were there this morning, were they not?"

"Yes. But they were on the floor under the chairs."

"So, as far as we know at this point, you were the last ones to leave the building and, therefore, the last people with an opportunity to remove the cash from the boxes."

Gabe rose from his chair and I put a hand on his arm. "Now see here …," he began.

Jake rose, too, and shook his head. "I'm just doing my job, Gabe. Look at it from my point of view. There are at least a dozen people who may have had a chance to steal the cash. I have to eliminate as many as I can." He sighed. "I'd like to take you and Miranda off the list. I don't believe for a minute that you took the cash." He paused. "But the fact is that you were the last to leave, the building was locked all night, and this morning the cash is gone. So you are suspects. You don't like it and neither do I. But there it is. I'll see myself out." He added with a wry grin, "I'd rather you didn't leave town. But I imagine you knew that."

Fifteen

The reality of being considered possible thieves hit us both hard. We sat in silence for a few minutes.

My slow burn was rapidly turning into a full rolling boil. "This is ridiculous!" I threw Gabe a fierce look.

He nodded. "Yep, but he's right, you know. The only way to prove that we didn't take that money is to find out who did."

"But we're fine upstanding citizens! I'm a librarian, for gosh sakes! You're retired FBI! We don't need the money! There's no motive!"

"There is that. But let's face it. Some people, when faced with money just left lying around, would not be able to help themselves, whether they needed it or not. It's an instinct."

"Well, it's not *my* instinct!" I replied in indignation.

"I know, love." He leaned across the table and took my hand. "And we were together, don't forget, we are each other's alibis, if it comes to that."

"Thanks a bunch but I don't want an alibi. I want to prove my innocence. It sounds absolutely ridiculous to even say those words!"

"I understand." He stood up and walked to my office just off the kitchen. He returned with a tablet and pen.

"So let's make a list."

"Of what?" I was still fuming.

"Actually," he said thoughtfully, "we need two lists. Who turned on the sprinklers and who took the money."

I was starting to regain my focus. "Ohmigod, they're not necessarily the same person!"

He smiled and nodded. "Exactly! But first, how about some more coffee?" He stood and refilled both of our cups.

I breathed out my frustration, hard. "And maybe a tranquilizer." I glanced at the clock. "And it's almost dinnertime."

Gabe has such a nice laugh. I had to smile at that point. We both know that no matter what the situation, we rarely miss a meal.

Harry joined us at some point; obviously, he also realized that it was almost dinnertime. But he sat down on the floor between our chairs. He had his own comments on our list. I'm glad no one was there to see us reading and writing names and making note of the cat's opinions. It went something like this …

"First list. Who turned on the sprinklers and why?"

"Right! Marcia Travis because she hated Lydia and wanted to ruin her quilt."

"Check."

"*Neooowww.*"

"Okay, make a note. Harry votes no on Marcia."

"Done. Second, maybe Laura Jenkins? I didn't actually see her there but general spite and on her cousin's behalf to ruin Lydia's quilt and as many other quilts as she could because they weren't hers."

"I can see that."

"*Neooowww.*"

"Duly noted. Harry votes no on Laura."

My phone rang several times and I ignored it as long as I could.

"Hello, Diane."

"I am so mad at you! You never call me."

"I've been too busy being a robbery suspect."

She took a breath and then giggled. "Oh Lord, I heard. That's hysterical!"

"I suppose it is if you're not the suspect."

"How can I help?"

"Gabe and I are making lists of people who would either turn on the sprinklers for spite and/or steal money meant for the school."

"Hmm, let me think about it. How about we meet up for lunch tomorrow? We'll compare notes."

"But, honey, you weren't even there."

"I certainly was. I was there with Ethan. Remember, I told you we were coming."

"Of course, I'm sorry I didn't see you."

"I saw you but you were busy at the front desk talking to Queenie so I didn't interrupt. There was a sign that said you didn't have to pay after 3 so we went right in. I didn't have a lot of time to get around before closing. Anyway, I overheard a thing or two. See you tomorrow at the Tavern at 1:00?"

"Sure."

"Hey, Mandy."

"What?"

"I'll be happy to be a character witness if you go to trial."

I heard her laughing as I clicked off.

We went back to our lists, this time with a glass of wine and a pizza on order.

"Who would turn on the sprinklers and why? Someone other than Marcia and Laura?" We looked at each other. We looked at Harry. Nothing.

"Think outside the box," Gabe advised. "Let's randomly say someone had a grudge against Queenie, didn't want the school to get the money, or hated the first-place winner?"

I looked at him blankly. "I got nuthin'."

He frowned. "It's just too wide a net. There were so many people there. It could be anyone with a grudge against anyone else."

"So, moving on, who took the money?"

"Let's start with the likelihood that someone triggered the sprinklers to distract attention away from them stealing the money."

I nodded. "Unless it was just a crime of convenience. Someone walked by and saw the cashboxes were unattended after everyone rushed away, and they couldn't resist it."

"Oh crap."

"Yeah."

"*Yeow*."

Sixteen

We woke up the next morning no closer to answers than we had been the night before. We'd eventually agreed that we had several hundred suspects and that I should see if Diane could shed any light on the subject.

I'd called Lucy late last night and told her I wouldn't be in on Monday morning. She'd heard about the money being missing and told me she would cover the library for as long as I needed.

I'd been serious when I'd told her I was ready to get back to my normal routine. I hadn't counted on an extended vacation at this point. I also decided to drink at lunch.

Although I'd invited Gabe to join us, he declined saying he'd use the time to return some business calls and maybe track down Kevin for a chat.

I slid into the booth and my cosmo was already there. She knows me so well. "Hey, you!"

Her face was solemn. "I don't know if I should be seen with you. Guilt by association and all that!"

I choked on my drink and she burst out laughing. "I've been waiting all morning to say that."

"Thanks."

"You look weary."

"Gabe and I have been trying to narrow suspects."

"For the sprinkler stunt, the theft, or both?"

"Yes."

She took a sip of her own cosmo. "Marcia or Laura?"

"They're our number one and two suspects, for the sprinklers, anyway." I added quietly, "Harry doesn't like either of them for it."

"Well, nuts." Diane was very familiar with Harry's ways, especially since the time he alerted her to my abduction with his caterwauling.

Lizzie sidled over to the table. "Afternoon, ladies. Two chicken caesars?"

"What's the special?" Diane asked, as she always did, although she never ordered it.

"Meatloaf, mashed, peas, biscuit." Lizzie stared out the window.

"I'll take that," I said.

Lizzie's eyes jerked back to me. "Last meal?"

Diane chortled and Lizzie grinned.

"You put her up to that," I accused.

Wiping tears from her big brown eyes, Diane raised a hand to protest her innocence.

Lizzie waited patiently. "You?" She looked to Diane, pen poised.

"Sounds good. Make it two meatloaf specials and two glasses of water, please."

She cracked her gum and looked straight-faced at Diane. "Taking you down with her, is she?" She walked away.

After we stopped giggling, Diane leaned toward me. "Anyway, back to the show. I got there around 3:00, just after the judging. That bargello was spectacular, by the way."

"I know." I felt a momentary pang at the way Amy had stormed off.

"Well, after the winners were announced, guess who I heard bitching!"

"Diane, please."

"Okay, fine. The second place winner was, uh, Violet Hempfield, right?"

"Sounds right. Gorgeous black-on-white whole cloth, all hand done." Then I added, "Right. I met her, nice woman, too."

"That's her. As it turns out, Violet's daughter Kate is married to …" She paused for effect.

I took a drink to keep from encouraging her.

"You are such a stiff. Dodgy Danvers."

I carefully set down my glass. "Get out!"

She smiled smugly. "I saw him there. Didn't you?"

"I was so busy with the raffle tickets, all I saw were hands and money."

"Well, first prize was a thousand bucks, right? And second place was $500?"

"That sounds about right."

She nodded. "I heard the announcements. Anyway, there was some general grumbling about machine-quilted pieces and hand-quilted pieces. Surely, you've heard that."

"I hear that all the time, but actually the National Quilting Association doesn't separate them for judging purposes."

"Well, they should, don't you think?"

I shrugged. "In my heart of hearts, yes I do. They're both skills but they're very different skills."

"You're not alone in that. And when Dodge found out that Violet came in second, he totally went off."

"Now wait a minute. Dodgy cares, why?"

"You just don't keep up, do you? After high school, Dodgy married Kate Hempfield and promptly moved in with her family."

That certainly fit with the Dodgy I remembered from school. His given name was Robert but he had been nicknamed after the Artful Dodger in Oliver Twist, courtesy of our junior English class.

He was known to steal fruit from the market when no one was looking and money from his own mother's purse on occasion. You never left any temptation in front of him and we all knew it. Lunch money was kept in many a sock because of Dodgy. Once we graduated, he became first-rate at dodging work and the nickname stuck. He never held a job that I knew of.

So he had married and moved to the Lancaster area in order to mooch off his wife's family, a move completely in character.

Our lunches were sitting in front of us when I came out of my reverie. Diane had the same look on her face.

We took a few bites of our delicious meals before we took up the thread again.

"So Dodgy has to be on the list."

Diane waved her fork at me. "Both lists. He could have set off the sprinklers because he was teed off that his mother-in-law didn't win. Then he might have taken the money just because he's Dodgy and it was there."

I nodded my agreement. "But Violet's quilt was still there when the sprinklers went off."

"Oh. Then that would be a crap move, even for Dodgy."

"But wait, I remember now, I talked to Violet after Gabe shut off the sprinklers. She had already packed up her quilt before the sprinklers went off. She was helping one of the other quilters pack up a soggy quilt when I talked to her." My eyes widened.

"There ya go. You definitely have to add Dodgy to the suspect list. He obviously waited until Violet got her quilt put away before he did it."

We ate in contemplative silence, partly thinking over our suspects and partly in mutual appreciation of the excellent meatloaf.

"Hey, what about the surveillance cameras?"

"What?"

"You are off your game, Sherlock! It's a government facility, for crying out loud. Shouldn't there be security cameras?"

My mouth fell open and my hand reached for my phone. "Gabe? Hi, it's me. Do you think there are security cameras at the Armory?" I paused.

Gabe was saying in my ear that he had already reached out to Jake on that. Of course, he had. But I saw no reason to rain on my friend's parade. So, when he asked me if I had just thought of it, I answered, "Diane came up with it. That's why she's Watson. Okay, get back to me."

I smiled at my friend. "Gabe said you're amazing."

"I know," she said with fake humility. "He's so perceptive, that guy."

After lunch, I decided it was time to show up at my day job. So I went to the library and straight to my office to get caught up. My in-box had a nice solid stack of paper in it, just what I needed to take my mind off the quilt show.

Lucy knocked and came in, minus her usual smile. "I'm so sorry about the show."

I looked up from my computer. "Thanks. Were you there?"

"Actually, I couldn't get away until about 3:30 so I didn't have much time to look around but the quilts were gorgeous, especially the ones with the ribbons."

"It was a great turnout and a wonderful show, until after." I said without looking at her directly.

"I bet you're making a list of suspects." She grinned at me.

I sighed. "There were just too many people around."

"Any idea how much money was lost?"

"I'm sure Queenie has a better number but, including raffle tickets, I'd guess close to $20,000."

Lucy looked like she might cry. "Oh no! That's dreadful. I guess I didn't think it would be so much."

That struck me as an odd thing to say so I waited for her to tell my why the amount mattered.

She sank into a chair in front of me. "If I tell you something, do you have to tell the police?"

"It depends, I think."

That seemed to be good enough.

She pulled out a tissue. "My younger brother, Jeff, was hanging around the front when I left. He, uh, had a rough time in high school." She rushed on. "But I thought he was doing better since he's been at the Tech School."

"I saw him there helping with set up." I added gently, "You don't trust him?"

She hesitated a second and then shook her head. "No. As soon as I heard there was money missing, I got this sick feeling in my stomach and I can't seem to shake it."

I sighed, went around the desk and put my hand on her shoulder. "Thanks for telling me, Lucy. We're trying to find surveillance footage and maybe that will put an end to this." I could feel her relax just a little. "How about we go get a coffee in the breakroom and talk there?"

"Thanks, Miranda." Her freckled face brightened.

I admit I didn't mind letting the last few days' worth of paperwork waiting on my desk. It was, in my experience, rarely urgent. And, after all, I was a robbery suspect! I smiled to myself as we walked downstairs, thinking about the conversation I'd have with Gabe later.

One of our part-timers was on the desk and we stopped for a quick chat with William, another English Lit major, unfailingly kind and thoughtful. I asked him how school was going and he asked me how Zoey was while Lucy listened in and waited for me. My purpose was twofold: I like William and I wanted to give Lucy a chance to relax a bit. Then some folks came up to the desk and Lucy and I moved on to the breakroom, which was empty.

We made our coffees and settled down. "Tell me about your brother," I opened.

She took a deep breath. "There's a big age difference. He's 19 now. I was in high school when he was born. Anyway, it's been hard for Jeff, having older parents. My dad is 63 and Mom's 59. It's hardly been an ideal household for a boy to grow up in. I went off to college while he was still in diapers. I can't say we're close."

I nodded but stayed quiet. I'm trying to learn when to let someone keep talking without interjecting. Something I've picked up from Gabe, I guess.

"Well, I saw Jeff at the show, hanging out around the front doors. It just looked odd, you know. And he didn't look happy to see me watching him either."

"Did you speak with him?"

"Sure. I walked right up to him and said, 'Hey, how's it goin?' or something and like that. He mumbled something and I could see he was anxious to be rid of me. That's what struck me as weird."

Then I remembered what I'd been meaning to ask Lucy. "Do you know a kid named Max who might be a friend of Jeff's?"

She shook her head. "No. I'll be honest with you. I don't think Jeff has many friends. He's always been kind of a loner."

I touched her hand. “Thanks for telling me what you saw. I think we should wait to see if Jake and the guys can catch whoever did this without dragging Jeff into it, at least for a day or two.”

“And you’re working on it, too, right?”

I chuckled. “I sort of have to. Gabe and I were the last ones seen near the cashboxes. As far as Jake is concerned, we’re his prime suspects.”

Seventeen

By the time I left at 5:00, there wasn't one paper in my in-box. The library runs smoothly, most of the time; I was lucky in that. I had the newest Freethy book tucked into my tote bag and things were looking up.

When I walked through the door, Harry had something on his mind. He was right there and I nearly tripped over him. He knows I hate that.

"Harry! Seriously." I took a step over him.

"*Meoww, neow, meow, wheo,*" he lipped off.

"Watch your mouth, you." I put my stuff down and then picked him up, which he doesn't particularly like either. "What's on your mind, buddy? Is this about the case?"

He laid a paw on my cheek and stared into my eyes. Since he was feeling so communicative, I asked softly, "Do you think the same person turned on the sprinklers and stole our money?"

He continued to look at me intently. "*Yeeoo. Yeeoo.*"

"Oh, Harry, really. It was premeditated?"

He placed his paws on my chest and pushed back. That's all he felt like giving me right now. I put him down. S*hoot.*

I looked in the refrigerator and found some breaded chicken cutlets and frozen broccoli. Close enough. I changed and then put the cutlets in the toaster oven.

When I heard the front door, I went to meet Gabe. It felt so natural and automatic that a tiny worry needled me. Was I getting too used to him being around?

"Hello there, sweetheart." He took me into his arms and kissed me soundly.

I pulled back, just as Harry had, to see his face. "Seems like you had a good day."

"And I can't wait to tell you all about it." He sniffed. "Cooking?"

"Oh, dear!"

I raced back to the kitchen and rescued the slightly overbrowned cutlets—nothing that a splash of jarred chicken gravy couldn't hide. I slid the bowl of veggies into the microwave and opened a bottle of wine.

Gabe set the table and we had our little meal in blessed silence, bracing ourselves for another evening of trying to solve these crimes.

I was clearing the table when the doorbell rang. The noise actually startled me. I swear to you that I go for months without ever hearing that sound. When Diane comes over, she comes straight in the kitchen door, usually without knocking. When Zoey comes home, she'll use her key or walk right in. Gabe parks his car in the driveway so it's easier for him to come in through the front, but he knows he doesn't have to knock.

I looked through the peephole and backed up. *Well, crap.* It was too late to pretend we weren't home.

"Hello. This is a surprise."

Laura Jenkins, paler than normal, cleared her throat. "I'm sorry to bother you." She spoke in a surprisingly subdued voice, but then I had only ever heard her voice raised in frustration or anger.

Another head, Marcia's, popped around hers. "May we come in?"

I stepped aside and opened the door wider, waving them into the living room, which is set up to accommodate two people and a cat. There is a small sofa against the side wall that rarely sees use and that's where they went. The two recliners are the main pieces, facing the wall-mounted TV. Harry had vanished from his usual spot. When Gabe was around, Harry had consented to let him use his recliner, provided he could sit on his lap, of course. I suddenly realized it was almost time for *Jeopardy*, darn it!

Gabe came into the room and I introduced him. He perched on the edge of a recliner and I did the same.

"How can we help you?" I inquired politely.

Laura burst into tears and Marcia patted her hand. Then she spoke for both of them. "It seems that people think one of us, or both of us in cahoots, I guess, turned the sprinklers on Lydia's quilt."

When she paused for a breath, Laura, dabbing at her eyes with a crumpled tissue, added, "It's awful. We went out to dinner last night and everyone stopped talking when we walked into Sylvia's. People walk by my house and stare. The looks I get. I don't want to leave the house."

"That's awful," I said and I meant it. Maybe I thought the same thing, but I wouldn't have flashed anyone a dirty look until I was sure. Others are not so particular.

Marcia nodded. "She's right. I want to go home but I hate to leave her here in this situation. That police chief of yours pulled his car right up in front of the house. I could feel the whole neighborhood watching and I don't even live here. He said I could go home as long as I didn't leave the state."

She paused and then continued. "I left the show at the end because I couldn't stand watching that woman flaunt her medallion quilt. So, when it hit 4:00, I packed up and left. Period. Laura came over to pick me up. I walked straight out the front door with my quilt bag." She took a breath. "I'd never deliberately ruin someone else's quilt, not even—"

I raised a hand to stop her. "Stop right there. It's not a fake, Marcia, and you know it."

She inhaled sharply. "Yes, I know."

Gabe, who had been listening quietly, intervened. "I spent some time with Chief Perryman today." He paused, choosing his words carefully. "Obviously, he can't disclose what he knows, but he's doing a great job. I think this situation will be resolved in just a few days." He smiled at the two woman and they both perked up. Those blue eyes always inspire confidence; I know that well.

"Honestly?" I turned to him.

"Yes, and I'm sorry I didn't have a chance to tell you. I talked to Jake earlier while you were at work."

Laura sighed. "Hopefully, he can clear me. I mean us, once and for all. I know I'm an easy target because nobody likes me."

Her cousin shot her a look. "No one likes you because you're mean."

"*I'm mean?* After you've gone around telling everyone that woman's quilt is a fake? Pot, kettle."

"You take that back."

Laura shook her head. "Pot, kettle."

I pretended to cough so I wouldn't laugh out loud. Gabe discreetly stared at the wall across from him.

Marcia stood up, ignoring her cousin. "So we came here to ask for your help, but maybe we don't need it after all." She had clearly inherited the family trait of blunt speech. Then she smiled and it looked like it hurt. "I didn't mean that the way it sounded. If you can do anything to move the police forward, we'd appreciate that. And thank you both for believing that neither of us did this."

The idea of telling them that Harry was the only one who had actually professed their innocence flashed across my mind but I had enough sense to keep my mouth shut.

Laura stood beside her cousin and now I could see the family resemblance. "That's right. Thank you for not thinking I ...," she touched her cousin's arm, "... that we, could ever do such an ugly thing."

Then Laura smiled. I'd never seen her do that before. It was rather disconcerting.

"You're welcome." And I left it at that.

As soon as the door closed behind them, Gabe had *Jeopardy* on and we got to play the Double *Jeopardy* round and final. Harry magically appeared for that, too.

The final category was World Geography so Harry and I pretty much conceded that one to Gabe. In all fairness, I was distracted.

When the show was over, we went back to the kitchen table, allowing Harry to settle in for his post-*Jeopardy* nap on the recliner, all to himself. He always found the show so mentally exhausting.

"You first," I said as soon as I took my chair and Gabe laughed.

"You got me."

"Yes, I did. Now tell me about your talk with Jake and why Laura and Marcia aren't suspects."

"Okay, when I got your phone call, I went straight out to the Armory and he was already there." He raised an eyebrow. "You know, he's not …"

"I know. He's not as dumb as he looks," I finished impatiently.

He looked surprised at my rudeness.

I waved a hand. "The whole town's been saying that ever since he was appointed. He knows it. It's not even news anymore."

He relaxed and grinned at me. "I believe that. Anyway, he and the Colonel were reviewing the camera footage. I know he didn't want to let me see it but I talked him into it."

A voice inside my head was screaming—"Get on with it!"—but on the outside I smiled encouragingly.

"The hallway camera caught someone holding a lighter up to a sprinkler. But it didn't get his face." Before I could interrupt, he hurried on. "It appeared to be a man. No rings."

My breath came out in a *whoosh*. "Oh, no."

"Yep, dressed in jeans, a sweatshirt, and ball cap, obviously trying to conceal his face."

"Okay."

"As for the cashboxes, the camera's screwed up in the front area." He sighed in frustration. "All we got were wavy figures. Of course, they're going to fix it now. But that won't help us. We need to find us some male suspects."

I flashed him a big grin. "I can do that." I filled him in on both Dodgy and Jeff.

"Nice work," he commented, after adding them to our list.

"So Dodgy (he couldn't say it without smiling) had double motives for the sprinkler and the money. If Jeff was involved he was probably the number two guy."

I nodded. "Lucy said he was nervous, hanging around, more likely the lookout than the brains behind the outfit." I paused. "I hate to think about it. Lucy'll go nuts." Then a thought occurred to me. "Hey, didn't we think it odd that the clean-up crew showed up so quickly? Remember, I said Queenie must have taken the time to call or had them scheduled for a certain time?"

"I do remember. And now that I think of it, first there were only two of them, and then suddenly they were all there." He patted my hand. "And by the way, Jake took both cashboxes to dust for prints. There are probably tons of them on there so I'm thinking that's a dead end." He added thoughtfully, "Let's take a closer look at the Tech School guys who were helping out first. We'll need to speak with Lucy's brother along with the rest." He gave me a concerned look.

I nodded and dialed Queenie's number.

"Hi, Miranda, I was about to call you. I'm letting each of the guild members know that there will be an ad in the paper on Wednesday."

I gestured to Gabe to pay attention and put her on speaker. "Okay, what ad?"

"I'm offering a reward for any information that leads to the arrest of those responsible for taking the money. I've reiterated that the missing money was for extracurricular programs at the school. Hoping someone will come forward to help us get it back. Surely there's someone out there who saw something or knows who took it. This is a small town and we basically know everyone who lives here."

"Oh, Queenie."

"Well, the way I see it, the front page is going to be all about the show and what happened anyway."

I couldn't argue with that. This was the story of the decade for our little weekly. "Of course."

"So I am hoping whoever took it simply saw it and couldn't resist and now maybe they're sorry."

"That would be good." I paused. "Queenie, taking another route, do you know who the boys were from the Tech School that helped out?"

"Oh, Miranda, surely you don't think …"

"I don't think anything at this point. Gabe and I are just checking out anyone we can think of."

The sounds of shuffling papers came through the line and then she came back on. "Okay, there was Jeff Huntley, Max Ryan, Terry Willis, and Dan Scott from the Tech School; Michael Smith, John Myers, Larry Johnson, and George Simon from the high school. I wrote down their names so I can send them thank-you notes."

I repeated the names so Gabe could write them down.

"Great." I felt awkward asking her the next question. "Uh, Queenie, did you call the crew to come back to clean up?"

"No, I'm afraid I wasn't that well organized at the time. But I had scheduled them to come back around 4:30 anyway. The Tech School van was to pick them up at the high school at 4:15 and bring them out to the Armory."

"Right, that's what I thought."

"Well, thank you for all your hard work, Miranda," she said softly.

"It's all going to be okay, Queenie, I know it will."

"One way or another." She took a deep breath. "The money we handed over to the boosters will take care of the band trip. They have to hire a bus and book their reservations fairly soon. So that's okay. But the football uniforms need to be ordered in the next week or two. So I've decided that if we don't get the money back, I'm going to give it to them out of my retirement account." Before the protest she knew was coming, she hurried on. "It's just not right, Miranda. They were counting on us. It's just not right." Then, without another word, she clicked off.

I turned to Gabe with tears in my eyes and took a couple of breaths before I spoke. Then I got mad. Then I made myself think.

"Gabe, Queenie asked the boys to come back around 4:30. We saw them, there were eight of them. But I saw two boys helping to clean up as soon as the sprinklers went off." I paused in my thinking out loud. "Some of the kids don't drive so there was a van bringing them all over and taking them home. So how did two of them get there early and why?"

Eighteen

After we'd spent another restless night, we were up early. While Gabe showered, I made the coffee. Then he pulled together a breakfast of bacon and eggs while I showered and dressed.

With each of us deep in our own melancholy thoughts, breakfast was a subdued affair. I had to pull myself together. Wallowing never did anybody any good.

"Well, getting back to my own life, I have to call Zoey."

His blue eyes crinkled. "I was thinking I should check in on Kevin."

I went into the living room and left him the kitchen while we called our respective children.

"Mom!" Zoey's bubbly voice poured out of the phone. "What the heck is going on down there? I saw a few things on FB from my friends in town."

"It's a long story, sweetie, but I'll give you the highlights."

I went on to tell her the briefest possible sequence of events over the last few days, punctuated by her gasps and cries of dismay. Finally, I paused for breath.

"You poor thing. Michael and I both feel just awful for you and your quilters. I'm glad Gabe is there with you."

"Thanks, honey. Me, too! He's been wonderful and he's working with Jake to try to solve this crime."

"Geez, Mom. Last year "The Quilt Ripper" and now this! Nothing exciting ever happened when I lived in Cutler!"

"And I was quite happy about that. Hopefully, we can get back to being the same boring little town very soon."

After we hung up, I took a deep breath, leaned back, and closed my eyes for a second. Gabe came into the room and sat down.

"Miranda, are you okay?"

"Absolutely. So how's Kevin?"

"Ladies first. How's Zoey?"

"Zoey just said, for the second time now, that nothing exciting ever happened in Cutler when she lived here. And I told her I'm ready for our boring little town to return to normal soon."

"I agree with that. Kevin is good. He said he and Terry had dinner a few nights ago with Zoey and Michael."

"Really? Zoey didn't mention it. But I'm so glad. Terry seems sweet."

"Kevin seems to really like her. She's also very driven. She's working on her doctorate in English Lit just like Zoey but I believe she's about a year behind. She's encouraging Kevin. So our kids are good and their parents are great!" He wiggled an eyebrow at me.

I laughed appreciatively. "You've got that right." I added, "But I do have to go to the library for a couple of hours. Do you have any plans?"

"I have some work to do, too. I handed off a few cases to other investigators and I need to check on them. I really hadn't planned an extended visit. And don't get me wrong, I'm not complaining." He reached for my hand. "I love being here with you."

I took his hand and squeezed it. "And I'm so glad you're here. Zoey was just saying the same thing. She apologized for not being here for me, but said she was grateful that you're here."

"Nowhere else I'd rather be." He said it quickly but his eyes met mine for just a second and I saw the truth in them.

I let go of his hand and stood. "If I'm gonna get to work, I've got to get going."

Gabe stood up beside me, "Before you go ..." He pulled me into his arms and kissed me. When we separated, I was breathless.

"Wow! I can't wait to get home now."

"I'll be here and I'll take care of dinner this evening."

Things were relatively quiet at the library. Those who did come in were talking about the quilt show and it was clear that the whole town knew about the missing money. I tried to stay out of the conversations but eavesdropped in case any names were mentioned.

Lucy was subdued and we didn't discuss it. That was fine with me because I didn't want to be the one to tell her that her brother was a suspect.

When I got home a few minutes after 5:00, Gabe proudly showed me the two beautiful Delmonico steaks he'd gotten at the market. He'd also gotten salad fixings and I volunteered to make the salad after I changed. I was hoping for a quiet evening at home for the two of us.

About 6:00, Gabe went out to the back porch and fired up the gas grill, which I rarely ever use because I'm the only one here. While he grilled the steaks, I started on the salads and munched a few bites as I chopped.

Gabe came into the kitchen and grabbed a couple of slices of cucumber and a stick of celery. "I'm starving. All this mystery and suspense sure makes for a good appetite."

"It sure does. How about a bottle of wine to go with those steaks, mister?"

"Done!" He went to the pantry to select a deep red burgundy, which I now know should be served at room temperature.

Dinner was delicious! And exactly what we both needed to refuel. We watched *Jeopardy* and then the baseball game that he'd recorded in the afternoon. It was a wonderfully quiet evening and I found myself wishing for more like it.

Nineteen

When the Wednesday morning paper came out, anyone in town who hadn't known what happened at the quilt show did now. I sat down at my desk at the library with a copy of the paper and a coffee. Gabe was going to track down Jeff and said he'd call.

We discussed calling Jake. Maybe we both felt a little awkward about not calling him, but we had nothing that came anywhere close to evidence. It wasn't a crime to show up early for work. There was no crime in being nervous. Jake had seen the same video footage that Gabe had seen.

I wanted to go with him. I really did. But the show was over and it was time for me to take back the reins of the library. Lucy had been a real trouper; but we had several events coming up, and I had to start doing my own job.

That doesn't mean I could resist reading the paper first. The headline screamed QUILT SHOW CAPER and clearly seemed to indicate that the sprinklers going off and the missing cash were part of a master criminal's plan. There were pictures of the dripping quilts and details about the cashboxes being left unattended. I felt my face flush as I read on. Gabe and I were the last ones out the door that day. I should have looked for the cashboxes more carefully before I left. I know Gabe felt the same. Maybe the thought had even crossed Queenie's mind but she'd never say such a thing.

In a box in the middle of the page was the open plea from Queenie for the return of the money. I said a silent prayer that someone would step up. How could anyone not feel bad about taking the money she described as earmarked for the upcoming band trip, new uniforms for the football team, and several other small but important school projects. With a population of 3,000, our high school senior class typically runs about 80 students. The band has about 40 members; the drama club about 20. We fielded about 50 football players but they had made districts last year. It was all small potatoes anywhere else, but not here, not if your kid was one of them; a college scholarship would go a long way.

I forced my attention back to the library but my mind kept wandering off to pray again. The missing money was a splinter in my heart.

My cell phone kept ringing and I mostly didn't answer it. I knew these folks were trying to get details out of me that the paper may have missed. I didn't feel like gossiping.

Then Diane called. "How ya doin'?"

"I'm okay."

"Sure, you sound terrific," she said sarcastically. "No word on the money?"

"Not yet. But you've probably seen the paper."

"It brought tears to my eyes. Poor Queenie."

"Mine, too." I took a breath. "Dee Dee, she's going to make up the money from her retirement account if it doesn't come back."

"No way!" I heard her sigh through the phone. "Well, that sucks."

"Yep."

"Okay then, moving on. I've had my nose to the ground over here. Remember I told you about Dodgy? Well, forget about him. I heard from a reliable source that his mother-in-law was so embarrassed by his behavior that she kicked his butt out of the show soon after the judging. No one saw him after that and his pickup was gone."

"Drat." I returned to the suspect pool in my head.

"It's okay, 'cause I heard something even better."

My ears pricked up. "Go on."

"There's a kid at the Tech School named Max Ryan. According to Ethan, the kid's trouble, big trouble, as in he should be in prison. He stole a car last year and tried to rob a Quickie Mart!"

"Seriously? What's he doing at the Tech School?"

"His family's Irish Catholic and their priest bailed him out by getting him into the Tech School and promising his good behavior. So they let him off with probation and kept it out of the papers."

"Very interesting."

"Isn't it?"

"I better call Gabe. He was going to speak to Jeff Huntley this morning. "

"Jeff? He's a sweet kid." She paused. "Maybe a little timid, but geez, I hope he wasn't involved. I've met his parents at several school functions."

"And you know Lucy's my right-hand woman around here. She's really important to me and he's important to her." I didn't know what else to say. "We'll have to wait and see, I guess."

"Catch you later. Call me if anything good happens."

"You got it."

I clicked off and immediately dialed Gabe.

"Hey, sweetheart. Nothing to report. I called the Tech School and Jeff is supposed to be in classes there today so I'm on my way."

"Well, I'm glad I caught you. Check out a kid named Max Ryan while you're there. It's possible he's the brains behind the outfit."

"Really?"

"Yeah. Diane just called and told me this kid is trouble." I paused. "He's already committed a couple of small crimes and should be in jail. I saw him the day of the show and I didn't want to jump to conclusions but I didn't have a good feeling about him being around Jeff." I added, "He's got mean eyes."

"Okay. I'm pulling into the lot now. I'll let you know."

"Gabe, be careful."

He chuckled. "Always. I'll call you later."

Twenty

When Jeff got up Wednesday morning, his parents were discussing the headline in the newspaper.

"What's going on?" he asked as he poured himself a bowl of cereal and got the milk out of the refrigerator.

"Someone robbed the quilt show at the Armory on Saturday. They took all the money that was supposed to go to the school to help out with the extracurricular activities and items that were cut from the budget."

"No way!" He kept his back to them. He had to pull it together.

"It says that someone turned on the sprinkler system and many of the valuable quilts got wet, including an antique medallion from the 1800s. That's terrible! Why would someone want to ruin those beautiful quilts and steal money from the school? I just don't know what's going on in this world of ours." Barbara Huntley read a little of the article directly from the paper. Bob was busy reading the sports pages and grunted his agreement.

"Yeah, that's terrible." Jeff sat down to eat his cereal, glad that both parents were busy with the paper.

He finished quickly and went back to his room. His head was spinning. They had agreed to keep cool for a few days before doing anything, to let the dust settle. Once the initial reports were out, everyone in town would be suspicious. Jeff had been a nervous wreck since Saturday and struggled to act normal, which wasn't easy. He got to school early and went looking for Max.

He found him where he usually was before class, standing outside smoking a cigarette.

Jeff walked up to him. "Hey, man. Where's the money? This crap is all over the papers, dude. Everybody knows!"

"Keep your voice down, fool! It's still in my car, just where I put it on Saturday. After school, I'll drive you home and we'll do the split, okay?"

Jeff lowered his voice. "Max, I've been thinking. We have to give it back, man!"

"Are you crazy? No way!"

"Listen, that money was for the school and they really need it. I just can't do it!"

"What about your mommy?" Max asked in a mocking tone. "You gonna go tell her to get lost? That you're not gonna help her?"

"Yeah, that's exactly what I'm gonna do. I can't help her, not like this."

"Well, you can do what you want with your share, man, but I'm takin' mine. I'm goin' to California. I'm definitely getting away from this dead-end town."

The bell rang and Max went inside, leaving Jeff standing there.

He tried again at morning break. Max was smoking outside again.

"Come on, Max, you know this ain't right, man! We have to give it back." He made the mistake of grabbing the front of Max's jacket. Max shoved him backward with his left arm and came up with a right cross to the jaw.

Gabe heard the yelling as he got out of his car. He spotted two young men in each other's face by the side of the building.

Then the larger boy hit the other one and the kid crumpled to the ground like a rag doll.

Gabe stayed next to his car and pulled out his phone. "This is Gabe Downing," he said quietly but clearly. "Please tell Chief Perryman he's needed at the Tech School on Hutchins Road. Thank you."

As much as he wanted to go check on the kid slumped against the brick wall, the other kid was moving quickly away. Trailing him carefully from behind parked cars, Gabe kept him in sight.

Suddenly, a Cutler police vehicle with its bright blue and yellow lettering pulled into the parking lot. The kid took off at a run.

Gabe turned and walked back to greet the chief.

"Timing's a little off today, Chief." He frowned. "Two kids had a fight at the side of the building." He nodded toward the boy slumped against the wall. "The other kid saw you coming."

Jake nodded. "Okay. Well, at least we got one of 'em. That gives us a place to start."

Gabe nodded and headed back to his car, thinking to let Jake handle the arrest.

Jake walked over and pulled the kid to his feet. The boy groaned but opened his eyes.

"How ya doin'?" The Chief looked closely at the boy's eyes.

"I'm … okay, I think," he mumbled.

"Hey, Gabe," the Chief called out.

At the sound of Jake's voice, he turned back.

"Can you hold on to this one while I bring my vehicle over here?"

"Sure." Gabe wrapped an arm around the boy who slumped heavily against him. "Doesn't look like he's gonna be any trouble."

Jake pulled his vehicle up close and together they wrestled the kid into the back seat. After he was belted in, Jake closed the door and turned to Gabe. "I'm gonna run him by the hospital. Might be a concussion."

Gabe nodded.

"Anyway, thanks for the call. You figure he knows where the cash is?"

"You can bet on it." He hesitated. "I overheard him say, 'We have to give it back,' right before he was decked. The other kid was about six foot, longish black hair, wearing a black leather jacket. Sorry, not much help."

"That's okay." He nodded toward the car. "Jeff's a good kid. I've known his family for years. I don't think he'll give us any trouble." The Chief drove away.

Gabe stood there for a minute, frustration seeping in. Ten years ago, he'd have caught that guy on foot. He was still burned over the incident last year when a college kid had gotten away from him, alias "The Quilt Ripper." He wasn't looking forward to telling Miranda that he had let another suspect get away any more than he was to telling her that Lucy's brother was about to be booked.

Meanwhile, Max made it to his car and waited until he saw the big white-haired guy and the Chief put Jeff into the back of the police car.

"Damn it!" he swore as he slowly drove away down the back road.

He drove slowly, obeying all traffic laws to the letter, back to his house and went to his room with the small blue duffle bag. His folks were working and his younger brothers were in school.

After he closed the door, he sat down on the bed and opened the bag.

"What the h—!?" He reached in and pulled a handful of shredded newspapers out of the bag. "That little creep! I'm gonna kill 'im."

It took him a while to calm down, but when he did he decided he had to find that money before Jeff gave it to the cops. Now where would he have hidden it? He wouldn't take it home. He'd never put his parents in that kind of spot. His sister's place? His school locker, maybe?

Max waited until the school day was over and drove back. He looked around and everyone appeared to be gone. One car was parked back by the cafeteria; he figured it was the school janitor. The old man was practically deaf and half blind so he wasn't likely to catch him.

Max hustled down the hall to Jeff's locker. It didn't take him long to open the cheap padlock with the hammer he'd brought from his car. He rummaged through the locker and there was nothing but a bunch of books and a jacket crumpled up in the bottom of it. He shoved everything back in and closed the door. He even arranged the lock so it looked like no one had been there.

He'd have to wait it out at this point. He knew where Lucy's apartment was but she'd probably be home from the library by now and he couldn't chance breaking in if she was home.

He drove by and sure enough, Lucy's little blue VW was parked in the driveway. He went home for supper. Now all he had to do was act normal until he could get that money back. And this time he was taking all of it.

Twenty-One

"Hey, Miranda."

I clutched the phone in a death grip. "Oh, Gabe, thank God. I'm losing my mind here. Any news?"

"Do you want the good news or the bad news?"

"You know how much I hate it when people say that. Okay, shoot. Start with the good news."

"We have a lead on the money and Jake Perryman has a suspect in custody." He paused. "He'll break down for sure and tell Jake where it is."

"Oh, that's wonderful." I grabbed a tissue as tears sprang to my eyes. I recovered quickly. "Okay, hit me with the bad news."

"The suspect is Lucy's brother, Jeff."

I sobered up immediately. "Oh no. Are you sure?"

"Positive. There was another kid involved and he decked Jeff before running away, so Jake took him to the hospital to get checked out."

"Oh, Gabe!" Tears filled my eyes again, but for a very different reason.

His response was solemn. "You should tell Lucy, Miranda, before someone else does."

I was rather, as my British friends say, gobsmacked but he was right. "Of course. Okay. I'll get all the details later. And Gabe?"

"Yes, dear." He waited me out, as if expecting another assignment.

Not sure if I got caught up in the emotions of the last couple of days, but it was at that moment when strong feelings surged through me and I couldn't help myself.

"I love you, Gabe."

The silence that followed seemed far longer than the three seconds it probably was and I started to feel like a fool when there wasn't an immediate response.

Then I heard him breathe out. "I love you, too, Miranda Hathaway. I've been waiting quite a while to hear you say that." His tone went from serious to joyous in the same mouthful of words.

I swallowed my tears and smiled. "Well, since you've been waiting so long, here it is again. I love you, Gabe Downing. And that's a subject we can 'discuss' later when we both get home." I heard him laugh as I clicked off and went to find Lucy.

It was a quick but hard conversation. I had to suggest she go over to the hospital and make sure Jeff was okay but also that he didn't say anything without a lawyer. Sure, I wanted him to tell us where the money was so we could recover it, but I didn't want Lucy's brother talking himself into a jail sentence without even trying.

As soon as Lucy hurried off, I asked Janie, who was on the front desk, if she wanted to call in some volunteers, but she assured me that she could handle it.

"I've got this, Miranda. And William is coming in at noon so he'll cover for my lunch break."

"Great, and have I told you lately that you're amazing. I don't know what we'd do around here without both of you."

"Thanks, Miranda." She blushed slightly.

I made a mental note to make a better effort to compliment my staff. I was probably a little lax in expressing myself and all three were totally dedicated, not only to the library but to me. Let's face it; the pay was minimal at best.

I went back to my office and called Diane. She had worked to solve the case, too, and she deserved to know. Plus, it would save me from another annoyed, "I'm always the last to know," phone call.

"Hey, Diane." I took a breath. "We have news."

"Ohmigod, just tell me."

"I will because I don't have the heart to torment you right now. Jake caught one of the kids who took the money. It was Lucy's brother. I don't have details yet."

"Wow, that's a surprise." She hesitated. "The other kid had to have talked him into it. Was it Max Ryan?"

"Well, I'd say the odds are good, but the second kid hasn't been identified yet or Gabe would've told me. At any rate, Jake has Jeff, who seems likely to spill his guts. I told Lucy to get to him fast and tell him not to talk until he has an attorney."

"That was good of you, considering he stole money from the quilt show you all worked so hard on. And, sure, I hope they get the money back for the school, but it's hard to think about Jeff going to jail. His parents will be crushed."

"I know. I hope they catch the other guy, especially if it is this Max kid, and throw the darned book at him."

A policeman sitting outside the door was half asleep. He glanced up and nodded as Lucy walked by. Jeff appeared to be sleeping. She looked down at him and a memory of the little boy playing with his trucks in the backyard flashed through her mind. She shook it off.

He appeared even paler than usual with his red hair a stark contrast to the white sheets. Lucy took a deep breath and touched his hand.

He opened his eyes. "Luce. Thanks for coming."

"Of course I came. How are you feeling?"

He swallowed. "I have a headache, and they tell me it's a mild concussion, but other than that, I'm good. Can I have a drink of water?"

"Sure." She lifted the glass from the bedside stand and put the straw between his lips.

He breathed out a sigh. "You're gonna be mad at me."

"Damn right, I am." She paused to compose herself. "Tell me why? Why would you do this?"

His eyes filled. "It was for my mom. My real— I mean, my birth mom. She's stuck in a crummy motel out by the airport, cleaning rooms so she can stay. The guy who runs it is a creep. I have to get her out of there."

"Mom and Dad …"

"She already asked them for help! They turned her away, Lucy." He took a deep breath. "She's counting on me. She doesn't have anyone else."

Tears sprang to her eyes but she brushed them away. "So you let this Max guy talk you into stealing."

"I think he would have done it anyway. I know that's no excuse. But all he talks about is getting enough money to get out of town." He stared at the wall.

"When I told him about my mom, he said he had a plan. And he could get me some cash for her if I helped. All I had to do was wait by the doors and keep watch while he took the money." He glanced sideways at her. "The hardest part was helping to clean up and acting like nothing had happened."

Lucy was torn between being angry and being disappointed. She wondered why Jeff didn't think he could have come to her. Maybe she hadn't been a good enough sister. True, the age difference was significant, and she'd been away at college and working while he was growing up, but she always felt that they loved each other. She didn't have a lot of savings but she would have helped as much as she could. *Or would she?*

A part of her would never forgive his mother for giving him up. She knew he was much better off where he was and all that stuff; but Ellie had gotten herself into this mess in the first place. It wasn't something Lucy would ever say to her mom; she'd have been crushed and would have lectured her about kindness and understanding. It was a lecture she'd heard before.

Don't judge him, she told herself, *just be his sister*. "So then Max took the money."

His voice sank to a whisper. "Yeah. He put it in a duffle bag in the trunk of his car." He coughed and asked for more water. She raised the glass again.

"Uh, I took it out and put in a bunch of shredded newspapers."

"You did what?" Her voice rose and the cop outside turned his head and looked in. Lucy gave him a wave and forced a smile.

After a few calming breaths, she said, "All right, so you have the money. You know that Max is gonna be looking for it, don't you?"

He nodded sheepishly.

"So where'd you hide it, Jeff? And don't even think about lying to me."

Lucy stepped outside the hospital and pulled out her cell phone. She couldn't go home. She pushed some numbers on her phone. Suddenly a man stepped from the shadows.

"Hello there."

She jumped away and turned to go back inside.

"Oh no you don't, sweetheart."

His arm went around her shoulder like a vise and he moved her away toward the parking lot. When they were out of sight between parked cars, he pushed her against a car door.

"Like they say in the movies, Lucy, we can do this the easy way or we can do this the hard way."

"I don't know what you're talking about."

"Don't waste my time. That wimpy little brother of yours has my money, and I want it. Now."

Lucy started to tremble. "I don't have it."

"Where is it?" His voice rose and he shook her.

"I'm not helping you." She said more firmly than she felt. "Turn yourself in, Max, don't make this worse than it is."

"What's worse than being stuck in this stupid town? I was going to cut Jeff in but now I'm taking all of it and I'm getting out of here for good."

"You won't get away," she said softly. The desperation in his face no longer made her afraid.

Several people stepped through the hospital's automatic doors and headed toward the parking lot.

"Let's go to your place and see if the money's there."

"No." She pulled away. "I'll scream."

He grinned down at her—and then pulled a hunting knife. "And if you do, I'll go back in there and make your little brother tell me where it is before I stick him."

"I don't think you're a killer."

He swallowed but his eyes were cold. "Wanna try me?"

Lucy made a decision. "Fine, let's go to my apartment and see if the money's there. Take it and run. See how far you get. Or we can just call Jake and have him meet us there and you can give yourself up. That's the smart thing to do."

He pulled her toward his car, opened the door, and shoved her inside.

Twenty-Two

After I'd put my tote bag on the hook inside the door and slipped off my shoes, I noticed that Gabe was pouring two glasses of wine, which was unusual before dinner. I felt oddly jittery and nervous all of a sudden.

"Hey, there! Any news from Jake?" I know, I know. I was making small talk to cover up my fit of nerves.

Gabe came to me and took me in his arms, "Oh, no you don't. You can't pretend you didn't say it!"

I pulled back and looked him squarely in the eyes. I put one hand on each cheek and pulled him down. "I love you, Gabe."

We came together in a wonderful warm kiss and we were both a little breathless as we separated.

He spoke first. "I know we've got a lot going on just now and we're focused on helping Queenie but we have to also realize that we're making a commitment to each other. I don't run around saying 'I love you' and I know you don't either. This is a very big deal for both of us."

"I know. We've been taking this relationship so slowly, each protecting the other and ourselves, but we need to stop doing that now. You're a wonderful man and I want you and need you in my life."

"You're making me blush," he teased, and then turned serious. "I agree. No more taking our time. I'm fully committed to you and this relationship."

He picked up the wine glasses and held one out to me. "I want to make a toast to our future, to our love, and to our lives together. I adore you, Miranda Hathaway."

We clinked our glasses and sipped. Suddenly, a mischievous impulse occurred to me.

"Hmm, Miranda Downing. What do you think?" I suggested.

Gabe's eyes widened.

I chuckled. "Don't look so stricken; I'm just kidding. We don't need to go from zero to a hundred in one day."

I stepped back into his arms and carefully removed the glass from his hand, "I'm thinking we should 'discuss' this a bit more before we get some dinner." I placed both glasses on the table.

He didn't respond in words, but instead scooped me up in his arms and moved down the hallway. I can't speak for him but I felt like a ton of weight had been lifted from my shoulders. I'd been in love for a long time but was afraid to commit too quickly for fear of scaring him away.

We came out about an hour later and scanned the refrigerator for food. "I'm famished. How about you?" he said.

"Absolutely famished."

"I think we're stuck with takeout or reservations. What do you think?"

"I don't really want to go anywhere tonight. Would it be okay if we just ordered a delivery?"

We were sitting at the table looking through my collection of takeout menus when my phone rang. I saw that it was Lucy and picked up.

"Hello?" All I could hear was background noise. It got my attention. "Lucy?" I said in a low voice.

Then I heard another voice and put the phone on speaker.

Twenty-Three

Jake sat down heavily, with a loud sigh, at my kitchen table. It was 1:30 in the morning.

I walked to the counter and filled a mug. "Coffee?"

"Thanks, Miranda."

I don't know when I've seen him look so tired. Although Jake was actually a couple of years younger than me, his weight and the mental and physical aspects of his job were taking their toll. I sometimes wondered how long he would continue in this position with all the stress it involved. But, with that being said, we'd seen more action in the past year or two than we'd seen in the previous decade. But was it going to stop? Ot were the times, as the song says, a'changin?

Gabe followed him in a couple of minutes later with an arm around Lucy, who was shaking like a leaf. She smiled at me as Gabe helped her to a chair beside Jake.

"Don't look at me like that. I'm fine, really," she said, although her teeth were chattering. "It's like a delayed reaction or something."

I went into the living room and pulled an afghan from the back of the chair and brought it to the kitchen. I wrapped it around her shoulders and gave her a quick hug.

"Thank you, Miranda."

"Would you like coffee?" I looked from Gabe to Lucy but they both shook their heads.

I grabbed a couple of water bottles from the refrigerator and handed them over. I noticed that Harry had joined us at some point at the table.

To my utter surprise, he put a paw on Jake's leg. Jake reached down, picked him up, and held him on his lap while he talked. It seemed so automatic that I'm not sure he realized he was doing it but I've never been prouder of Harry.

I forced myself to focus as Jake started to talk. Gabe and Lucy listened quietly as well. Although it was clear that we were all exhausted, it appeared that nobody was going to get much sleep.

After we called him, Jake went straight to Lucy's apartment. I glanced at Gabe, who shook his head slightly.

Jake continued. "I saw them pull in. I let him go in and settle down. When I was sure he'd relaxed his guard, I stepped in and grabbed him before he had time to react." He managed a tired smile.

"So Max is tucked away in a jail cell and I'm headed home to get a few hours' sleep. Ron's guarding him. He was on call tonight anyway. Tomorrow, we'll put all the pieces together and wrap it up."

We all looked at Lucy.

"I could only pray that you heard me through the phone. I heard you answer and …" She actually giggled. "I put it back into my pocket without thinking."

Now we all stared at her in disbelief.

"No, really. I wasn't being clever or anything. I was just so surprised when Max grabbed me …"

We all laughed then and I think it was mostly in relief that Lucy had accidentally allowed us to overhear her conversation with Max.

After a moment while we gathered our thoughts, Jake gave Lucy a serious look. "Do they know the rest of it?"

She flushed and shook her head. "No, not all."

He looked at her for a long second and said quietly, "Well, might as well tell them, Lucy. It'll be in the paper and on the news by tomorrow night. They deserve to hear it from you." He stood and gently placed Harry on the floor with a final pat on his soft head. "I'm gonna try to grab a couple hours of sleep."

Lucy started to cry.

Gabe and I walked Jake to the door.

"What a mess," he said sadly. He shook hands with Gabe. "I know you were there to back me up. Thanks for letting me take him down."

Gabe nodded with a small smile. "You're the chief."

"*Yeow.*"

He glanced down. "Thanks, Harry."

Gabe closed the door. We walked back to the kitchen and sat down. Harry apparently felt that he had exerted himself sufficiently for the evening so he grabbed a snack kernel or two and sashayed toward the bedroom.

"Maybe you'd better start over, Lucy," Gabe said quietly.

There was a soft knock on the front door. Lord, we hadn't had this much action in, well, never. I glanced at the clock above the sink. It was 2:10 a.m.! Gabe answered it.

"May I come in?"

He walked into the kitchen followed by an older woman: blue eyes, red hair with a few grays streaked through it.

Lucy must have heard the voice because as soon as the woman stepped through the doorway, Lucy bolted to her.

"Mom!"

The woman hugged her daughter close. "As soon as we heard what was going on, we came home." She pulled back and gently touched her daughter's face. "I've just come from the hospital. Dad, of course, is in his workshop pounding things."

"Please sit down, Barbara. Can I get you something?"

"A glass of water would be great, if you don't mind."

Mother and daughter sat side by side.

"I'm glad you're here, Mom. I was about to explain about Ellie. But you know more about that than I do."

Barbara took a sip of the water I'd placed in front of her and sighed. Her face appeared to grow more tired and sadder right in front of us. "Yes. I knew Ellie was back in town. I should have been here for Jeff." She cleared her throat. "I should probably start at the beginning."

We gave her a moment to gather her thoughts.

"I was in school with Ellie's mother, June. She was a sweet woman but a little … soft. She married a local man, Ed Swifton. He was, excuse me, a right bastard, that one. He ran her life with an iron fist. Poor June had no life outside the house. The only time she ever left it was to go to the grocery story. When she had Ellie, she spent most of her time keeping the child out of his way."

Tears filled her eyes and she looked at me with shame. "He was too loose with the belt. There were many of us who knew it and did nothing. It's easy to say things were different then but there's no excuse. I kept in touch with June but all I did was drive her or Ellie to the Emergency Room from time to time. I should have done more.

"As soon as Ellie turned sixteen, she ran away. She took up with a man named Jay Jessup." She shook her head. "He was a bum and about twice her age. She soon found out that he was cut from the same cloth as her father and a mean drunk. She learned to stay out of his way mostly, especially once she got pregnant. But then one day, he twisted her arm until he broke her wrist.

"After she got back from the ER, she waited until he fell asleep and shot him." Barbara took another drink of water. "There were a number of people who cheered when she did it. But none of them were on the jury and her lawyer was a drunk himself. Everybody knew that, too." She cleared her throat. "They sentenced her to 20 years for premeditated murder."

I was truly horrified. "Oh no! How could I not have known about this?"

She smiled at me sadly. "Unbelievable, isn't it? Well, it wasn't such big news in Cutler because they lived in Elmera at the time. Her parents were here, of course, but certainly didn't advertise it and she had broken contact with them completely. There were two or three of us who visited her upstate while she was there. It was a poor excuse for doing the right thing, I know. So, when she asked me to take her baby, it was a chance to do something for her.

"I pretended to be pregnant for a while and told everyone how embarrassed I was about it at my age. She didn't want her parents to have the baby, you see. They never visited her so it was pretty simple. She gave birth to Jeff, I went and got him, and she spread the word that her baby had died. No more than a handful of folks knew different."

She patted Lucy's hand. "Bob and I kept this secret to ourselves for a long time. Then when Jeff graduated high school, we felt that we owed him the truth. So we told him and Lucy about Ellie." She swallowed. "It was hard. He went to see her a few times."

"I can't believe you could keep a secret like this in Cutler!" I exclaimed.

Barbara smiled. "It sure helped that he was a ginger, like Lucy and me."

She squared her shoulders and raised her chin. "Anyway, a couple of months ago, Ellie was up for release and I was concerned. She'd never said anything about coming back to Cutler but where else would she go?

"So, when she showed up, at least Jeff wasn't taken totally by surprise. And I think you know the rest. We turned her down when she asked for money, but she contacted Jeff. He went out to some dive motel on I-80 and she told him if he could get her some money, she'd move to Mexico and never bother us again.

"Of course, Jeff thought it would be better for all of us if she left town, so he told Max what was going on and Max came up with the idea of stealing the quilt show money. Jeff went along for a share." She ran a hand through her hair and now tears splashed down her cheeks. "I'll never forgive myself. If we'd given her some money, she would have gone away and he wouldn't be in this terrible mess."

Lucy took her mother's hand and squeezed it. "I should've stopped him."

I raised a hand. "Now wait a minute. Coulda, woulda, shoulda! We'll all do what we can. There has to be some good to come out of all this suffering. There are too many victims here. At the end of the day, there has to be justice."

Twenty-Four

Lucy went home with her mom to spend the night. Gabe and I realized that we'd never had any dinner and each ate a bowl of cereal before we went to bed. I tried to get some sleep but the extent of pain this family had been through weighed heavily on me. Eventually, I moved over closer to him and he put his arm around me without saying a word so I knew he felt it, too.

The next morning, way too early, we dragged ourselves out to the kitchen for coffee. Talking things through as we tended to do, we made yet another plan of action. With a pad and pencil on the table in front of us, Gabe made the first call just after eight.

He called Jake to find out exactly what Jeff and Max were likely to be charged with and whether both boys had legal representation. Jake told Gabe that Max's family was already working on his behalf. We both knew that Max had been in trouble before, so they probably had a lawyer to contact.

Then I spoke briefly with Barbara.

"Good morning, Barbara. Sorry to call so early."

"Not a problem, I've been up most of the night and I want to go see Jeff first thing."

"Is Lucy up yet?"

"No, I'm letting her sleep in. This whole thing is such a nightmare."

"I know and I'm so sorry for all of you. Listen, let her sleep and when she gets up tell her to take the day off. I've got things covered at the library."

"Oh, gosh, Miranda. I'm so sorry. With all this going on, I completely forgot that it's Thursday morning and she should be at work. To be honest, when you're retired like Bob and I, you lose all track of days and dates. I'm so sorry."

"Now the first thing you have to do is stop apologizing. None of this is your fault." I hesitated. "I don't mean to be pushy but I was wondering if Jeff has an attorney or if you have one in mind."

"No, not yet. I suppose we need to find one today."

"I'd be glad to make some calls."

The relief in Barbara's voice was palpable. "That would be such a help. I can't thank you enough."

"No problem. Try to get some rest."

She took a deep breath. "Thanks, Miranda. After I see Jeff and find out what's happening maybe I'll be able to rest. I'll be talking to Ellie, too."

"Oh."

"We're going to do the right thing. We should have before. If she wants to stay in Cutler, we'll help her get a place to live and a job."

I had to gather my thoughts for a moment. "Really, that's quite kind of you, considering …"

"We made a mistake, a selfish mistake, and now Jeff is paying for it. Thank the Lord we can still make amends."

I truly didn't know what to say.

She helped me out, saying softly, "I'll tell Jake that you're working to get Jeff an attorney."

I cleared my throat. "Okay, sounds good. Now I've really gotta run. Talk soon."

As much as I hated to do it, I had to go to work so I proceeded with my cereal and fruit breakfast. I showered and got dressed and returned to the kitchen. Gabe was sitting at the table tapping on his laptop.

I walked up behind him and put my arms around his shoulders. "Have I told you lately that I love you?"

"Isn't that a song?"

"Yes, it is and if you want I'll sing it for you but it might spoil the mood." He pushed back his chair and pulled me down onto his lap. After a proper morning kiss, I stood up.

"I've got to run. I want to be there by 9:00 so William and Janie don't think they've been deserted. But I can make some phone calls from the office once I make sure everything is running smoothly."

So I went off to work. As soon as Janie and William arrived, I told them Lucy wouldn't be in and not much else. They assured me they were expecting a quiet day.

I went to my office and made my first phone call. I'd gone to high school right here in Cutler with Harold Michaels and, frankly, he was the only criminal defense lawyer I knew. But when I called, he said regretfully that he was already representing Max. His only recommendation was an attorney from Lancaster that he'd known in law school.

As I was pondering my next move, my cell phone rang and it was Zoey. She said she'd called the house and spoken briefly with Gabe. She said all of her FB friends from the area were posting stuff about the quilt show caper and that someone had been arrested.

So I spent half an hour bringing her up to speed. She said all the things I was feeling and then some. She was aghast but also angry at the miscarriage of justice Ellie had suffered. But that still didn't give her the right to come back to Cutler and cause problems for the people who had helped her. And it certainly didn't give her the right to put her son in such a terrible position. By the time I got around to the part about trying to find an attorney for Jeff, she was on board.

"Wait, Mom, I can help with this! Have you forgotten that Olivia's an attorney?"

"Oh my, I guess I had. But she's in Boston with you, right? And isn't her specialty corporate law?"

"Well, sure, but she'll talk to some of her associates to find a good Pennsylvania defense attorney who's interested in fair play. Sounds like they're pretty scarce around Cutler."

I chuckled at her indignation. "Thanks, Zoey. I'll leave this in your capable hands then." I paused, "Just try to bear in mind that we're not real deep in the pockets around here."

"No problem. I'll bet there are a couple of attorneys out there who will do it pro bono!" She took a breath. "Don't worry, Mom, I got this. I'll call you back this afternoon."

"That's a great relief. Thanks, sweetheart."

I hung up thinking how lucky it was that Zoey had called and remembering all the times the kid had said to me, "I got this." From the first time she rode her bike to the end of the driveway and back, through every challenge all the way through to college and beyond, it was her mantra. Always scared me a little, but she was right every time. So, when the kid said, "I got this," I knew I could move on to the next task.

Of course I called Diane. She was annoyed at having missed the late night powwow.

"Stop right there," she said as I began to unravel the story of the Huntleys. "Tell me over lunch at Sylvia's. I want to hear it all. You're buying."

"I figured."

I called Gabe. "Hey sweetheart, Diane wants to have lunch. Are you okay with that? Can I bring you something?"

"No, no, you go right ahead. I'm actually making some calls and answering some emails about new cases. I'm gonna have to do some work eventually, but you can tell me all about it tonight over dinner."

"I will. See ya later."

New cases coming up! My heart sank a little when he said that. But of course he had his job to do and his job was in Boston. If this whole nightmare with the quilt show hadn't happened, he'd have gone home on Sunday night like usual. I was foolish for letting myself get used to playing house with him when I know full well my life is in Cutler and his is in Boston. Saying 'I love you' hadn't changed that.

Lunch with Diane always improves my mood. I have some good constants in my life, I reminded myself. She said she wanted to eat first and listen later so we munched our roasted chicken salads in silence.

As I wrapped up the whole story, her eyes narrowed. "Let me know when you find out who the judge is."

"What?"

She grinned. "Sweetheart, my family connections go way back and, frankly, so do yours. We also need to find out if the D.A. is going to handle this himself. I would think so. Hmm, John Tyler." She smiled a Grinch-like smile."

I flushed. "That was a very long time ago."

"Ah, but you're so unforgettable, Miranda."

I sighed. "Can I go to jail for this?"

She chuckled. "Looking up an old friend? Nah." She tapped her fork against my plate. "The way things are going for these people, someone needs to render justice that's a little less blind." She winked at me. "Or, to put it another way if you prefer, we're going to grease the wheels of justice a little."

Twenty-Five

Judge Bridget McAllister sat behind a large desk in her private office, tapping a pencil on her blotter. Jeff sat behind a small table in front of her, with District Attorney John Tyler in a chair on his right, and his attorney, Tara Williams, on his left. She was young, blonde, and in a light blue designer suit. There were two rows of chairs arranged behind them.

Gabe and I were seated in the second row, trying to be inconspicuous. Jake slipped in and sat down beside me. The judge stopped tapping and sat up straight.

"Very well. Ms. Williams, welcome to my court. I have received your appearance. It is my understanding that you have a deal with Mr. Tyler here," she nodded at the D.A., "in exchange for which your client is pleading guilty to criminal mischief, and criminal conspiracy charges pursuant to section 903 of the state criminal code are being dropped."

The young woman stood. "We have, Your Honor."

"No need to stand, but thank you."

The young attorney immediately sat down without a word.

Tyler nodded his agreement. "We have, Your Honor."

"Mr. Huntley, do you understand the implications of agreeing to this deal?"

Jeff raised his red eyes to the judge. "Yes, ma'am," he said in a whisper.

"Speak up, son," she said, not unkindly.

"Yes, ma'am," he replied more firmly.

"You may address me as 'Your Honor.' Very well, I want to be sure that you understand the severity of your crime before I agree to this deal. You are admitting to a third-degree felony, that of criminal mischief, which is punishable by up to seven years in prison and a $15,000 fine."

Jeff's eyes went wild and he looked at his attorney desperately. She laid a restraining hand on his arm and shook her head slightly, willing him to be quiet.

"However, due to your lack of previous conviction, the state has agreed to a sentence of two years' probation and a weekly check-in with a parole officer for the first three months, after which you will have monthly check-ins with that officer." After a moment, she added, "I am also adding a requirement that you attend the Scared Straight program at the state penitentiary as soon as that can be arranged."

She paused and sighed. "Do you understand and agree with these terms?"

A tear slid down his pale cheek, but he nodded then said clearly, "Yes, ma'am, Your Honor."

"So be it." She nodded to the attorneys. "The plea is accepted and so noted."

As Jeff rose, she gestured him to step forward. He stood in front of her desk. In a gentler voice, the judge addressed the young man. "Jeff, I've known your family for years and I can't begin to tell you how much it pains me to see you here. I can only imagine what Bob and Barbara are going through." She glanced back at the first row where Barbara, Bob, and Lucy were seated all holding hands.

My eyes followed hers, except I couldn't stop looking at a slender woman with light brown hair seated beside Barbara.

The judge fixed the boy with a steely gaze. "I want to believe that you're a good kid but easily led astray and lacking in judgment. I encourage you to stick with the Tech School and find something useful to do with your life. I don't want to see you again." Without missing a beat, she added in a louder voice, "If I do see you in this Court again, I will throw the book at you. Are we clear?"

He swallowed, hard. "Crystal clear, Your Honor."

She managed a small smile. "Then get out of here."

The following day, Judge McAllister took the bench in her courtroom, formally dressed in her black robes, and stared severely at those seated at the front tables. The bailiff called the court to order with his pronouncement: "The Court of the County of Montour is now in session, the Honorable Judge Bridget McAllister presiding!"

The judge cleared her throat and looked once more at the paperwork in front of her. "I have reviewed the submitted motions." She shuffled her notes. "Let the records show that the charge related to conspiracy to commit malicious mischief has been withdrawn and the defendant is charged with a single count of theft. Due to the nature of the crime, this is a second-degree felony pursuant to sections 3921-3934 of the state criminal code. How do you plead?"

Howard Michaels rose at once. "To a single count of theft, my client pleads guilty, Your Honor."

The judge looked oddly disappointed. She took a long look at Max, who swept his long hair out of his eyes and met her gaze.

She nodded, almost to herself. "As the defendant has stipulated as to his guilt in this matter, I am prepared to proceed to sentencing in this case without further delay."

The defense attorney stood up with his mouth open. The judge froze him with a glance and he sat back down. She looked to the D.A., who nodded grimly.

"The defendant will stand."

Max stood defiantly.

The judge met his eyes and frowned. "Have you anything to say for yourself?"

"I just wanted to help Jeff. He asked me to help him," he said loudly.

The judge put her hands together as if in prayer. Then she sighed. "I don't believe you, Max. You come from a good family but we both know you've caught a few breaks already or you would have been in juvenile detention a long time ago."

The boy's defiance appeared to wane. "Yes, Your Honor."

"It seems we have failed to impress upon you the importance of staying out of the system. So now you will be in it for some time. I hereby sentence you to six months in the county jail to be followed by six months of home confinement with ankle monitor. This will be followed by two years' probation during which time you will report in weekly to a parole officer," she said in an ominously quiet voice.

His eyes wide, Max looked at his attorney. Howard shook his head.

I looked at Mr. and Mrs. Ryan, who were seated in the front row along with the priest from St. John's. As soon as I looked, I wished I hadn't. Mrs. Ryan was crying softly. Her husband had placed his arm around her.

The boy's shoulders fell and he started to sob.

The judge addressed him one more time. "Max."

He wiped his face with his hands and forced himself to meet her stern gaze. "Yes, Your Honor."

Her eyes bored a hole through him. "I want you to hear your mother crying and take a good look at her face. Remember this day, son."

He sniffled, but nodded.

"It may not seem like it but this is a lenient sentence. If I ever see you in this Court again, I will throw the book at you. Are we clear?"

"Yes, Your Honor." Max repeated.

"We thank you, Your Honor," Mr. Michaels answered quickly.

The Judge rose and banged her gavel. "Adjourned."

Twenty-Six

"Ladies, come to order." Queenie tapped her pen against the glass pin jar on the table in front of her. That sounded much better than tapping her scissors against her water bottle and she smiled.

"I'm not going to belabor the events of the past week or so. We were all present for them. I do want to thank each and every one of you for your heroic efforts before, during, and after the quilt show."

She paused as she has been known to do and glanced at her notes. "The amount that we raised has now been confirmed at $19,759. The first part of that, $4,000, was used for the band trip arrangements and I understand that the remaining amount will be returned to us soon." There were a couple of gasps and a few claps of appreciation. She acknowledged that with a smile. "But we do have one piece of unfinished business. The winner of the Husqvarna machine is …"

Darn her dramatic pauses, she was killing me here. I wanted it, I wanted it, I wanted it …

"Laura Jenkins."

What? What? I was thinking it but then someone said it out loud.

"What?" *Oh no. Was that me?*

Everyone looked at me. *Oh Lord, I said it out loud.* I shrugged an apology.

Queenie cleared her throat. "That's right. I have invited Laura here today to accept delivery of the machine."

I hadn't noticed Laura coming in and hadn't heard the bell. I wondered if she'd been waiting in the back room.

Queenie waved a hand and Laura stepped forward.

"Thank you all. This isn't easy for me." She spoke in a softer tone than we had ever heard before. "I'd like to ask Queenie to help me repair the family quilts that I've inherited."

Eyes were wide and mouths were open, mine included.

"And I would like to leave the machine here until she can help me learn to use it properly." Her eyes went to the floor. "I'd like to be a better quilter."

The silence continued.

Then Queenie stepped up. "So, ladies, my thinking is that we would ask Laura to join us next Saturday for our charity project." She peered at her Post-it Notes on the table. "We are scheduled to make pillowcases for the children's ward at the hospital. I think we can teach her that quickly and it's a nice start. Can I see a show of hands?"

Laura's face went pink and she refused to look at us.

Okay, we're a bunch of softies, we quilters. All hands went up.

"Thank you. By unanimous vote, Laura, you are invited to join us next week."

She put a hand out and Laura shook it. She made an effort to smile at us and then bolted for the door.

The wheels of justice were grinding too slowly for us. The court case had been decided on Thursday and we all knew that Jeff had hidden the money at Lucy's apartment. *So where is it?*

As if in answer to my mental question, the bell above the door jingled. We all turned to see Jake and Gabe walking in.

"Good afternoon, ladies," Jake said.

Gabe wandered over to my side and pulled out the stool next to me. When he sat down, I reached for his hand, hoping no one else noticed.

After a chorus of "hellos" and "heys," he continued, "Queenie, on behalf of the Cutler Police Department, I am pleased to return to you the funds from the Guild's quilt show, since they are no longer needed as evidence." He hoisted a small duffle bag onto the nearest cutting table. He fumbled around in his pocket and pulled out a notebook. "I'll need you to sign a receipt for me."

Our fearless leader appeared frozen in place, afraid to move from the stool she was seated on. But Brittany, our little pepper pot, jumped up and said, "Thanks, Chief."

She took the receipt book and put it in front of Queenie. We scrambled for a pen and she put that in Queenie's hand and told her to sign.

"Uh, I should also tell you that the amount being," He looked at his receipt, "$15,759, the guys at the station and, uh, other places nearby, chipped in $201 to make it an even $16,000."

At the sound of our heartfelt applause, followed by Brittany jumping up to kiss his cheek, the chief beat a hasty retreat.

Trying to get Queenie to grasp the reality, Brittany opened the bag and placed it in front of her. She put a hand on her shoulder. "Look, honey, we got the money back!"

Queenie visibly relaxed. She took a deep breath and a smile started to find its way to her face.

"Yep, it's really back." Brittany gave her a hug that finally shook her out of her shock.

She looked at all of us with tear-filled eyes. "I can't thank you all enough. For your work on the show and for …" Her eyes met Gabe's and then mine. "… for getting this money back." She picked up the bag and clutched it to her chest. "Oh my, I think I'd best go to the bank."

"I'll go with you." Brittany popped up, grabbed her quilt tote, and they headed for the door. Gabe looked at me and I nodded.

Gabe hurried after them. "Ladies, wait. I'd feel better if you'd let me drive you."

When the three of them left, the rest of us sat down on our stools, basically speechless, which I guarantee doesn't happen very often. Someone passed the box of tissues around. I took one as it went by me. It was a good feeling to know that promises made could now be kept.

Twenty-Seven

I got home before Gabe and noticed his suitcase sitting beside the door. I took some iced tea out of the refrigerator and piled some cookies on a plate before sitting down at the table.

When he came in, I offered him a glass. He sat down across from me.

"You're leaving?"

"Yep. I've got some things to tend to at home. I've gotten a couple of calls from potential clients and I really should follow up in person. And I left Kevin in charge of the house, so who knows what shape that's in by now."

We both knew what that meant. While Kevin was getting better, his standards of order were no match for Gabe's. I managed a smile, envisioning an empty refrigerator, hampers full of laundry, and piles of mail.

I nodded. "How's Kevin's job search going?"

"He's interviewing. It takes time."

"I'm so happy for him."

I meant it. Kevin had lost his way a bit after college and grad school and Gabe had suffered right along with him. Last year, Zoey's fiancé, Michael, had given him a business card and I'd rather hoped he'd seek him out about job possibilities. With his master's degree from Penn State in Business Administration, it was a perfect fit. But his stint at running a coffee shop had led him down another path. After some discussion and debate, he decided he'd like to run a hotel. We were thrilled that he was moving in a specific direction, even if he had to start at the bottom and work his way up.

Gabe interrupted my thinking. "I don't really want to go so I was wondering ..." It was unlike him not to finish a sentence. Gabe was a clear thinker, if nothing else, so he had my attention.

"How would you feel …?"

I looked at him curiously and I swear he blushed! "Like I tell my kids at the library, sweetie, use your words."

He smiled at that. "Thank you. Okay, I was wondering if you'd have any interest in, or you would at least think about, me moving to Cutler permanently."

There are very few times in my life when I am speechless, let alone twice in one day. I sputtered and gasped for a couple of seconds. Then I composed myself. From his expression, I could tell his uncertainty was rapidly changing to misery at my lack of an immediate response. That's the problem with two quick thinkers being together.

I put a hand on his across the table. "Gabe, I would love that."

He had apparently been holding his breath because I heard a slow release. "Are you sure?"

I nodded and took a deep breath of my own. "This year has been hard on both of us. And we've been through a lot together in a relatively short period of time. I also know I'm the one with her feet in cement. I don't want to leave Cutler. It didn't seem fair to ask you to be the one to leave your home in Newton." I stood up and walked around to sit on his lap. I put my hands on his cheeks. "But since you brought it up …"

He hugged me tight. When we separated, he said, "Now, if you're not ready for us to actually live together, I can probably get my apartment back at Vinnie's."

I was profoundly touched. "Don't be ridiculous." I felt my chin rise. "If you're moving here to be with me, you're going to be here with me." Uncertainty crept in fast. "Unless you don't like it here."

"Man, this is hard, isn't it?" he said quietly. "We're both so afraid of making a mistake. Honey, this house is fine with me as long as you're in it."

Harry had mysteriously appeared at that moment and was shamelessly wrapping himself around Gabe's legs.

Gabe reached down and petted his furry head. "And Harry, of course."

We smiled at each other for a minute, and then he pressed on. "So here's what I was thinking, now that we're clear on that. I know you need a little time to settle down at the library and all. So I'll go home and start clearing out stuff that I don't need from the house. Then, in a couple of weeks, maybe you could come and help me pick out anything you'd like to have from the house and I'd bring a few things down here."

Wait. What? Oh. He was going to actually move his stuff here. Logically, that seemed only fair, but I liked my house the way it was. "Okay."

He laughed at the expression on my face. "What I meant was maybe I could bring my leather recliner."

Suddenly, we were both aware that Harry was sitting on a kitchen chair next to Gabe, listening intently.

"Then I wouldn't have to take Harry's chair all the time." He turned his head slightly, addressing both Harry and me.

Harry gave him an enthusiastic "*Eeow*." Then, to my astonishment, he raised a paw in the air and Gabe gently met it with his palm.

"Was that a high-five?"

"Yep. We've been working on it."

"Oh, for heaven's sake. It's starting to feel like two against one around here."

Just as I said it, Harry jumped from the chair to my lap. He reached up and placed his paw on the side of my face. The face thing was his most affectionate gesture.

I petted his head. "Thanks, Harry."

He jumped down and went back to the living room. Clearly, his work was done.

"And I was thinking I'd let Kevin stay on in the house but I'll keep paying the expenses until he has a secure job, if that's okay with you."

I took a breath. After all these months of going slowly, the blending of our families was now moving at a breakneck pace. I was getting dizzy.

"It's your house, Gabe. You can do what you want." We had never discussed finances.

"Miranda, this wouldn't impact our travel or other plans in any way. Financially, I mean."

This habit of reading my mind was a bit disconcerting. "I didn't mean … I wasn't going to ask …" I babbled.

He looked at me intently. "As soon as we get our living situation in order, we should sit down and review our finances, to put your mind at ease."

I exhaled slowly. "This is a bit much for me all at once." I stood up and Gabe joined me. "So, to recap, you're going home to prepare to move. I should make room here for some of your things. Then I'll come to Boston and we'll decide what to bring down. And in about a month or so, you'll be here with me for good."

"Right."

I reached up, stood on my tiptoes, and put my arms around his neck. "Okay, I think I'm just gonna bask in the glow of that last part for a minute or two."

Gabe pulled me into his arms. "Basking is one of my favorite things." He whispered into my hair, "Let's bask awhile before I leave." He released me but took my hand and led me back the hallway.

One of my last coherent thoughts for the next hour or so was—*Boy, I'd better call Diane—tomorrow*!

Meet the authors…

Photo by Jackie Rhule

Debbie Devlin Zook and Mary Devlin Lynch are sisters who have been avid readers since childhood and now share a passion for writing. Living in different states has made the sisters' collaboration quite a challenge but it has also brought them closer together.

Debbie lives in central Pennsylvania. She's retired and loving every minute of it. When not writing, she is a reader and avid sports fan. She is also addicted to several TV shows like *NCIS*, *Castle*, and *Bones*. Debbie has one son, Scott, who lives with his wife, Wendy, in Rochester, NY. She has two grandchildren, Zack and Addie.

Mary lives in the Bronx, New York City. She recently retired, but that hasn't slowed her down. She's a notorious multi-tasker combining quilting and writing with reading two or three books at the same time. She also runs her husband's business in her spare time. Mary has one daughter, Megan, who lives with her husband, Peter, in Natick, MA. She has two grandsons, Collin and Luke.

Beth Devlin-Keune

Beth Devlin-Keune, the youngest Devlin sister, lives in Cape Coral, FL. With her Administration of Justice degree, her insight has been helpful in several chapters of this book. This is the second book she has collaborated on with her sisters. Her life revolves around sports and animals. She was a member of the Penn State softball team and has coached several teams. She is currently renovating and flipping houses in her area. Naturally, she is also a voracious reader. Beth and her partner of 25 years have two dogs and several cats.

Other Books by the Devlin Sisters:

The Witherspoon Adventures:
Beautiful Disaster (Magee) Book 1
Burnt Roses (Melissa) with Beth Devlin-Keune Book 2
Before Everafter (Madison) Book 3
Relative Unknown – Sequel

Cayden and Cat Adventures:
The Wright Move, Book 1
The Wright One, Book 2
The Wright Woman, Book 3

Meredith Abbott Adventures:
Lying for a Living: Meredith Abbott's Adventures in Hollywood (1)
Dying for a Headline: Meredith Abbott's Adventures in England (2)

Miranda Hathaway Adventures:
The Quilt Ripper (#1)
The Missing Quilter (#2)
The Quilt Show Caper (#3)

A Hollywood Designer Adventure:
Sophie By Design

E-mail: devlinsbooks@gmail.com
Facebook: devlinsbooks
Twitter: @devlinsbooks
Blog: www.devlinsbooks.com

Made in the USA
Monee, IL
04 May 2024

57966451R00105